QUEEN
OF
SWORDS

OTHER BOOKS BY ANNE ELIOT CROMPTON

QUEEN OF SWORDS

ANNE ELIOT CROMPTON

Methuen, New York

Library of Congress Cataloging in Publication Data

Crompton, Anne Eliot.
Queen of swords.

Summary: An unmarried teenager, estranged from her parents and her
boyfriend, struggles to provide a future for herself and her year-old son
that does not include welfare.
[1.   Unmarried mothers—Fiction]   I.   Title.
PZ7.C879Qe   [Fic]   79-26496
ISBN 0-416-30611-X

Manufactured in the United States of America by
Fairfield Graphics, Fairfield, Pennsylvania
Designed by David Rogers

First Edition

Published in the United States of America by

Methuen, Inc.
733 Third Avenue
New York, New York 10017

QUEEN
OF
SWORDS

Now

I know the way home.

Any morning I can walk out onto State Street and up State to Main and take the bus. The bus comes every half hour, and it rumbles up Main to Federal, and up Federal till the houses spread out and some yards have trees. Then it passes a big sign, Welcome to Mechanicsville. That's my hometown.

Any morning I can step off the bus at the corner of Jackson Street; and the second house down on the right— that's home.

The second house on the right is a red clapboard, two-story. Dad's pickup is parked out front, with two-by-fours sticking out. The living-room curtains are lace, and right now you can see a Christmas tree through the lace.

I can stand on Jackson and look at the house, and then I can start up the walk. And the door will fling open, and Mom. . . .

Any morning, this can happen.

Or maybe I should call first—just in case.

IMAGINARY CALL HOME

(The phone rings several times. Mom is taking her hands out of dishwater. In the living room, Dad hides behind Field and Stream, *pretending he doesn't hear.)*

MOM.	Hello?
ME.	Mom?
MOM.	Susan? *Susan?*
ME.	Mom, it's me. *(I can hardly talk; my throat's so tight.)*
MOM.	Darling, where are you?
DAD	*(in background).* Is that Suki?
MOM	*(calling wildly).* Dan, it's Susan!
ME.	I'm pretty close, actually. I'm in Springerton. I was wondering if I could come see you, Christmas and all. . . .
MOM	*(crying).* Susan dear, are you . . . is he . . . ?
ME.	I'm alone.
MOM.	He left you?
ME.	Nine months back.
MOM.	You've been alone for nine months! Why didn't you call?
DAD	*(close in background).* Here, let me talk!
ME.	Well, actually, I'm not really alone. I—
MOM	*(a dangerous edge in her voice).* Are you telling me—
ME	*(hastily).* Oh, no, no, no! Not a man, Mom! But I've got Jason.
MOM	*(still dangerous).* Who's Jason?
ME.	My son.
	(Mom gasps. In her silence, Dad takes over.)
DAD.	Suki!
ME	*(crying).* Merry Christmas, Dad.
DAD.	He left you, right?
ME	*(humbly).* Yes.
DAD.	What's this, you have a baby?
ME	*(barely able to speak).* Yes.
DAD.	Then holy Pat, why aren't you home now?

4

ME.	Oh, I was so hoping you'd say that!
DAD.	Where are you? I'll come get you.
MOM	*(in background).* They can live home—tell her.
DAD.	You can live home, you and the kid.
ME.	Well, actually, I'm leaving—
DAD.	Leaving for where?
ME	*(finally getting hold of myself).* I won the South Beach Design scholarship.
DAD.	South Beach Design . . . that place in California you were thinking about before?
ME.	That's right, and I have to take the bus out the sixth. *(And I'm trembling from hair to toes, hoping you'll want to keep Jason home with you. He's your grandson, after all!)*
DAD	*(slowly).* Well. I'm proud of you, Suki. You must be pretty good, winning a scholarship without even high school. *(He really does sound proud!)*
ME.	I won it with a portrait of Jason.
MOM	*(in background).* Tell her the baby can stay! We'll keep him.
DAD.	You hear your mother. *(I sure do!)* We'll talk about that when we're all together. Now tell me where you are.
ME.	Springerton. One one four State.
DAD	*(disgusted).* That slum! Get your stuff together; I'll be there in half an hour.
MOM	*(in background).* Tell her I've still got the crib and the playpen. Everything's down cellar!

Any day this can happen. I can walk over to Ahmed's Bar on Main and call home. Only I never do.

5

December 24, Evening

In my room at home I had a plaster statue of the Virgin Mary. Mary wore a white robe and veil, with a blue mantle; and I had painted little blue flowers on the hem of the robe, and little white flowers on the hem of the mantle. Mary held out loving arms, and while she didn't exactly smile, her expression was sweet and accepting as though she might smile soon.

My only friend, Rianna, has a statue of Isis in her room. Isis wears a horned crown and no veil. Her long hair ripples free. She has a flowing robe and mantle like Mary, and her expression is sweet and accepting. She stands in the middle of the round table in the middle of Rianna's room, and at her feet stands an open box marked Offerings. Rianna keeps a five-dollar bill in the box, so her clients will think they have to put in at least that much. That way it's legal; it's a religious contribution or something. The clients don't pay Rianna; they pay Isis. Telling fortunes for money is illegal.

My only friend, Rianna, is a witch. I thought witches were supposed to be ugly, but Rianna is a handsome woman. She's a bit older than me—maybe twenty—and tall and slender. She wears long flowing skirts and caftans; and when she reads your fortune with tarot cards, she winds a black turban over her long black hair. Rianna reads tarot cards for a living, but she does mine free.

Tarot cards are dreamlike pictures. They show you everything that can happen in your life—things you worry about, things you want, things you didn't think of yet. They show marriage, children playing in gardens, happy homes; sickness, murder, misery; love affairs, accidents, law problems; money, no money.

Rianna spreads all the cards face down on a blue velvet cloth, and I pick mine out. "Slowly, Sue. With your left hand, remember."

"Oh, yes." I switch hands. "Why the left?"

"So Isis can guide you. You control your right hand too much."

When I've picked them all, Rianna turns my chosen cards over and lays them out like a cross and reads them.

She touches a card called The World. It shows an embarrassingly naked lady dancing happily inside a Christmasy wreath. "The World says travel, also success. You're definitely going to California."

But I know that! Nothing in this world could keep me here! I've accepted the scholarship, and I'm definitely off on the sixth of January—Epiphany—to the bright land of opportunity, oranges, and earthquake.

"This is your past—where you have been," Rianna says. She touches a card that shows two beggars, one gaunt, one lame, stumbling through snow past a lighted window. "But that's all right; that's behind you. You've been there already."

I sure have! I'm still there, actually. But before me is The World, the South Beach School of Design, and sunshine. There's just this one small problem. . . .

"And here's The Empress again. I don't quite get that."

The Empress, a rosy earthy lady, rests comfortably on a red-cushioned seat in a bright garden. Her flowing gown is white, red-embroidered. A waterfall splashes nearby, and flowers like jewels hide in the grass. Loosely The Empress holds a scepter tipped with a ball. Beside her leans a shield with the device ♀ . The Empress' full lips are silent; her eyes are grave; and stars shine in her hair.

Whenever I pick The Empress, Rianna has trouble reading her. She usually says, "I don't quite get that," or "Well, it's kind of obscure," or "Let's see the next card."

Now she shrugs and turns to the next card. "Ah, here we have your old friend, Sue—The Queen of Swords."

Most times I pick this ferocious queen. It's weird. With seventy-eight cards to pick from, I almost always manage to slip this one in—altogether and entirely against my will. The Queen of Swords is a dark, fierce lady. Rigidly she grasps an upright sword. She sits straight and angular, and her profile is colder than her stone throne.

Rianna has no trouble reading her. "She is rejection, Sue—abandonment. You have been rejected."

That's hardly news. I've been rejected for sure! Paul is hitchhiking now in Spain or maybe Italy, with Amy. They're picking oranges or stomping grapes, or whatever they do there. As Rianna taught me, I send a hate thought after them. I touch them with hate—I feel my hate make contact—and then I feel a bit better. Paul isn't the only one who can reject!

"But before you now," Rianna repeats, "is The World, travel and success."

But there is still that one tremendous small problem. Right here and now, it tires of being good. It reaches up and yanks on the velvet cloth and says, "Zuzu? Awa!" ("Susan, I'm lonely, cold, hungry, tired, bored—pay attention to me!")

Rianna's lip curls. I reach down and grasp Jason's warm, stocky body and haul him up onto my lap. Clasping his dark, curly head to my breast, I ask her, "What does Isis say I should do about Jason?"

For I can't take him with me. I can't wrestle him across

the country on a bus, change and feed and bathe him, and keep him quiet enough so the other passengers won't strangle us. When I get there, I can't keep him in a dorm. I can't take him to class—he'd have a great time yanking down easels—and I can't afford a sitter. Right now I've got $37.42 in my jeans pocket, and I feel rich! I can't afford to just not go, and stay here with him, either. That way I'd be on welfare forever—no good to either of us.

"What about Jason?"

Softly Rianna touches The Queen of Swords. "Sue," she says, "it's Christmas. Have you called your folks?"

"I've been thinking about it." Wanting to! Every time I walk down Main I think of home. The stores play Christmas music, and I remember Dad singing with his friends around our Christmas tree. Under the tree always stood the Christmas crèche. Dad carved the three holy figures when I was Jason's size, and Mom painted them. Much later, I repainted them.

"Do they know about Jason?"

"No."

"They might love him. Folks are funny like that, especially around Christmas. Do they know Paul's gone?"

"No, they don't."

"Tell them."

My Mom is a beautiful dresser. She has her hair done at the Parlor, and her pastel pantsuits are always fresh and smell of lilac. That's what she does for herself. Everything else is for us—I mean, was for us. Maybe Rianna's right, and Mom would love Jason. She might say, "It isn't his fault, poor little lamb!" and run down cellar and haul up the playpen, even if I didn't go to confession. I think of Mom in a pink pantsuit and apron, rolling ginger cookies, and I want . . . I want so much. . . .

Rianna murmurs, "People get soft at Christmas. Hell, it's worth a try."

9

I stand. I sit Jason back down on the chair and snatch up my coat. Jason shouts, "Awa!" and clutches at me, but I step away quickly. He doesn't like to stay with Rianna, but it's only for half an hour.

"He can stay," she sighs.

"I'll be right back. Can I take some change? It's long distance."

Rianna nods at the Offerings box. Isis and I do business; she gets my dollar bill; I get her dimes and quarters. I don't want to call collect; my folks might not accept the call. This way they'll hear my voice first, and I'll make them glad; I'll make them glad!

I mustn't cry in front of Rianna, who has no illusions. "I'll make it snappy," I tell her. And I say to Jason, "I'm going bye-bye. Stay with Rianna."

"Awa," Jason says. Then he yells, *"Maaa-maaa!"* "Awa" is his first word of protest. If that doesn't work, he tries *Mama*, a forbidden word. It used to get a reaction from me—"No, Jason, not Mama. *Zuzu*"—but not anymore; I've learned better. Now I just ignore it. Jason wails as I run out to the street.

Snow blows in my face. One good thing about snow, it cleans up the street. Overflowing garbage, dog shit, cars parked on three wheels—the new snow hides all this. Under the blue streetlights I see just blue-white everywhere.

Snow slips into my sneakers as I stumble past lighted windows. Some have modestly drawn shades. One shows me a frank view of two fat men drinking beer in front of TV—might make a good beer ad, sketched in heavy pencil or charcoal—another frames a small fake Christmas tree.

Up on Main the Christmas lights loop from pole to pole. "Aunt" Millie's house is on the corner, number 70. Rianna and Jason and I are going there Christmas—unless I'm home by then! It feels good to know someone, to guess who is washing dishes behind the kitchen shade. Even out here I hear kids squalling and a man shouting.

That'll be "Uncle" Stan. He's a short-tempered man, and I can't blame him with all those bratty kids. Only one of them is his. The rest are State kids, foster kids that Aunt Millie takes in. Rianna says she does it for the money. Could be, but she's an awfully good mother to them!

Lisa, the oldest, is Stan and Millie's real daughter. Suppose Lisa had a lover, and Stan and Millie found out. Would they throw her out on the street? Not a chance! Though they're religious, like my folks.

I turn the corner onto Main. In the front window their Christmas tree leans as if it's looking out. It's a wild tree with the tinsel thrown on as if the kids had had a tinsel fight. As I go by, it shakes, and a star falls off.

AHMED'S says the red light blinking on and off, two blocks down. I head for it, winking away dumb tears. I'm seeing our Christmas tree at home—not so wild as Aunt Millie's, but homey, informal—and the crèche right under it. I see the Baby reaching out tiny hands to the world, and Mary and Joseph kneeling in cotton snow. For most of my life I believed the Baby Jesus was God, come into His world by a miracle. That was Christmas.

I am working against a tide of shoppers. All the stores are open, blaring Christmas music, and the shoppers are desperate. Just this evening left! A thin man scampers past, only his legs showing under his load of packages. A woman drags a crying kid by the wrist. She whirls and slaps it, yelling "Shut up I'm sick of you!" and I wince. Anxious faces appear out of the snow and fade back into it. I know what they're thinking— "Will he like it?" "Can she return it?" "My feet are killing me!" "Holy Pat, I forgot the milkman!" "Time for a drink."

I have bought nothing for my son. That's all right; he'll

never know. Santa Claus is not on his short word list. For Rianna I have bought a hand-turned mug with herbs painted around it. Rianna is herb crazy and tea crazy. I had to buy her something; for nine months she's been my only friend, and she is certainly the best friend I've ever had. And together we are going to take a bottle of Chianti to the Aunt Millie Christmas dinner.

Ahmed's is dim, except for the string of lights in the window. Five men hunch over the bar. They all turn and look at me as I come in. I walk quickly to the back. If I don't look at them, they probably won't speak to me. There are rare times when I am glad to be a bit dumpy, with mousy, short hair. This is one of those times. From the corner of my eye I see the men swing back to their drinks, all but the last man. He is black, middle-aged, hefty. He is still watching when I reach the phone.

Ahmed's has no booth, no book or light. Just a phone on a shelf. Before I can stop to think what I am really doing, I pick up the receiver and pop my dime. It takes a bit of dialogue and a mighty fumble for change, but I get the number. I hear the phone ring at home.

It rings and rings.

They must be home. This is Thursday night. Mom is taking her hands out of dishwater. Dad is hiding behind *Field and Stream*. . . .

A loud, nasal voice says abruptly, "Hallo!"

It's like a jab in the ribs, that strange voice. Breathless, I ask for Mrs. O'Hara.

"Wrong number," says Nasal decidedly. "No O'Hara here. Wait a min." Someone speaks offstage. "O'Hara used to live here. Moved."

Now I am having trouble breathing. "Do you know where?"

"Nah." Click.

Slowly I hang up. I lean against the shelf and try to

think, and tears dampen my hands. I'm crying. O'Hara moved. My folks moved. To Chicago? Mom had a cousin there; I don't remember his name. San Francisco? Dad used to talk about moving someplace warmer. He also talked about Ireland, where he had never been. When the oil bill came, he'd shout, "It's enough to send a man back to Ireland!" Mom's sister in Rhode Island might know. What's her married name? But maybe they just moved down the block. How do I find out?

Someone is standing beside me. It's the black man from the bar. He asks, "Something wrong?"

I draw back from him. Then I see he's not just middle-aged; he's as old as my Dad. And he looks kind. I tell him, "My folks have moved, and I don't know where to."

"Well," he says, "wouldn't hurt to try Information." He looks at me sharper. "What's the name?"

"O'Hara."

"Plenty of O'Haras."

"Daniel Sean O'Hara."

"That's more like."

He pops a dime and dials. He is kind! I didn't know what I was doing, and he must have seen that. He talks to Info, nods to me: "Get this down." But I have no pencil, paper, nothing. Jamming the receiver between his chin and shoulder, he wrenches an envelope out of his pocket, and a pencil stub, and scrawls. He hangs up, rips off the scrawl, and hands it to me. "You're in luck. They didn't move far." It's still a Mechanicsville number. I can hardly see it through my tears and the dim light. I look up to thank him, but he's gone back to the bar.

Again the phone rings and rings. They can't have gone out! At last the receiver lifts and I hear my Dad's voice, slow and lilting, which I haven't heard in two years: "Hello?"

ME (*gasping*). Daddy!

1 3

DAD (*unbelieving*). Suki?

ME (*very fast, before he can hang up*). Merry Christmas! I just called to say Merry Christmas! (*His voice turns me back into a little girl. I feel the way I did the time I got lost in New York on the school trip, and I managed to call home, and I heard his voice like now and I felt safe, though he was a hundred miles away.*)

DAD. Suki, where are you?

ME. I'm in Springerton. I'm alone, Dad.

DAD. He walked out on you?

ME (*humbly*). Yes.

DAD. Can you come here?

ME. I was hoping you'd ask me! But I'll be bringing my baby.

(*A silence follows, just as I have always imagined it. I can hear Dad breathing. The operator cuts in, and Dad switches the call to collect.*)

DAD. How long have you been alone with a baby?

ME. Nine months. Jason's a year old.

DAD. Holy Pat!

ME. Dad, is Mom there?

DAD (*after a moment*). Suki, I'm in the same boat as you.

ME. What?

DAD. Your mother's gone.

ME. What? (*Mom can't be dead! Oh, no!*)

DAD. Walked out.

ME (*it is my turn to gasp, to fall silent and gather up my brains*). Do you have her number?

DAD. No. I've tried. No number. Look, Suki, I live at sixty and a half Oak now. Can you find it? I'd come get you, but I sold the pickup.

ME (*numb*). I can find it. When?

DAD. I won't be here Christmas; I'm real sorry. I work the next day. How about Sunday? Can you come then?

14

ME. What time?

DAD. When you can; I'll be here. *(Doesn't he go to Mass?)* Suki, it's been great to hear you. Just wonderful!

ME. Me, too.

DAD. Just in case, where do you live?

ME. One one four State.

DAD. Good night, Suki, sweetheart.

ME. Good night.

At the bar my friend is talking to another man. He has his back to me. I would like to thank him, but I don't want to attract attention at that bar! I leave a dime by his hand and walk out without speaking. I'm not sure how my voice will sound anyhow.

Back at 114 State, Jason is asleep on Rianna's narrow bed behind the screen. He lies curled up, soft cheeks damp, thumb in mouth. We talk softly.

"I knew it," says Rianna, "the Queen of Swords!" She points to the cards still spread on the velvet cloth, bright in the lamplight. "You're still abandoned, Sue."

"But my Dad's going to see me."

"Kid, your Dad's not going to take Jason off your hands!"

Well, no, I guess not. But he *is* there at 60½ Oak. I have heard his voice; he is going to see me. I still have a kind of home.

I wrap Jason in my coat for the trip up the cold stairs, and he wakes and snuffles and asks, "Zu?"

"Going bye-bye," I tell him. "Going home."

"Um." ("I'm happy I'm with you.")

"Keep the faith," says Rianna. "We'll think of something."

Think of something. Sure—and quick! Here it is the twenty-fourth, Christmas Eve, and I have to leave on

January sixth. One thing I know—I'm going. *Nothing* is going to hold me here!

Up in our room I snap on the overhead light. Our room is almost bare. We have a camper-size refrigerator, and a hot plate. We have a queen-size mattress with a sleeping bag on which we sit and sleep. And we have a radio on the floor by the mattress. I turn it on first thing, and it croons. I like the sweet-music station, LUV. Paul always listened to classical.

There are neat ways you can furnish a place without money. Rianna made a couch out of crates and homemade pillows. Paul made a file for his photos out of crates. I don't bother. If I'm going to be creative, I'm creative on paper. Our peeling walls are covered with my best pictures. Well, no—my second best, actually. My best were portraits of Paul. There was a charcoal nude, all slim, sleek tension, so beautiful it embarrassed me. For Paul was—is—beautiful. He has Jason's springy brown curls and dark eyes, and a body to melt a girl's heart on sight. Holy Pat, I never had a chance! Even if I had known what was coming—even if I had known Rianna then, and she had read my cards—I could never have turned Paul down. There were other portraits. I drew Paul hanging proofs, Paul chopping salad, Paul listening to music, head thrown back, eyes wide. All those I threw away. The portraits looking down on us now are of Jason, of Rianna, and of Aunt Millie. And I have a watercolor of Mom, which I did back in high school.

Mom is standing in the front door, looking out, with her back toward us. She's resting one hand on the doorframe and looking away, casting a shadow back toward us. I like that very much. I love the way the blue pantsuit blends into the blue shadow. And I never wondered before why I had painted Mom with her back to us!

Maybe I was telling myself something in that picture. I

do tell myself things in pictures, like in dreams. (Maybe Tarot cards are the same trick. Maybe it isn't Isis telling you at all, but yourself telling you. I'd like to think that.)

When you are mixed up, when your heart is tired of feeling, then you do your special comfort thing: Mom knits; Rianna makes a slow, aromatic tea; Paul listened to classical; I eat.

I love spaghetti, also lasagna, macaroni, ravioli, chili—anything satisfying that comes in a can I can heat on my hot plate. Rianna warns me I'm getting fat, and it's true. I had to buy size 14 jeans last time. But, holy Pat, so what? I'm not looking for a man. I've had enough of that game to last me . . . well, quite a time. First thing I do tonight, I set a can of spaghetti with meatballs to heat in the saucepan with Jason's aba ("bottle").

Then I put Jason down on the mattress and change him. We use disposables, and I don't feel guilty. That's all I need to do—wash diapers! Sister Teresa back at Holy Name would say, "That's the least you can do, Susan, and offer it up!" But I've learned from Rianna to call that masochism—an altogether dirty word. (Some day I'd like to get Rianna and Sister Teresa together; watch the fur fly!)

Jason smiles and chuckles sleepily. He lets me peel off his shirt and wrestle him out of his favorite elephant-patch pants without a murmur. For bed he wears a soft flannel nightgown with blue roses.

Dinner is served. We sit together on the mattress. First I spoon applesauce into Jason's small, pink mouth. When he turns his head away and waves his hands No! I give him his aba. He holds it himself; and now I can wallow in spaghetti and meatballs.

Oh, the comfort of spaghetti! It's as if I had a red-checked tablecloth and candles instead of a bare dusty floor. I feel almost as if I have wine, and maybe even a good friend to share it. It's wonderful! But it doesn't last long. The can is empty in seconds.

I wash up our mess in the corner sink, and munch stale lettuce. Rianna says I should take vitamins the way I did when I was nursing Jason. But I priced them at Main Drug yesterday. Forget it!

We sleep together under the sleeping bag. I'm taking it to California with all my stuff rolled up in it. "Um," says Jason, and curls against me.

I watch the reflections of car lights sweep across the walls. I listen to shouts from the street, and an argument out by the bathroom.

Where is Mom? How many cold, dark miles separate us? Why, after some twenty years of meals and laundries and Sunday Mass, did she walk out on Dad? Will I ever see her again? Dear Lord, will I ever see her again?

I try not to say my prayers at night. It was a firm habit I had, but Paul said it tied me to my past and my folks, so I tried to break the thread. But even now, when I'm really mixed up, prayer comes natural.

I try to reach out to Mom across the unknown distance, to touch her with love the way Rianna has taught me. My own will, my own energy, can carry love—or hate—to the target; there's no need to bring God into it. I send Mom love on the force of my own energy. My will flies like a love-tipped rocket, searching for her. It falters. It comes back to me. It can't find Mom.

So I whisper into the dark, "Our Father who art in Heaven." And I feel my energy swallowed up in God's energy. God knows where Mom is.

Jason sleeps. I move my hand to touch him and sink.

Christmas Eve Remembered

We always left the house together at eleven thirty. Whatever the weather—rain, sleet, snow, moonlight freeze—we walked together up Jackson to Federal and down to the corner of Tyler, and St. Patrick's Church. On Federal we joined the crowd of walking shadows. At Tyler the crowd thickened; they came from all directions, families together, old men bent over canes, young couples holding hands. Cars nosed around the corner into St. Pat's icy parking lot. Overhead, St. Pat's bells clanged.

The church seemed to welcome us in. Stained-glass windows glowed softly. Outside the door the Christmas crèche was lit. This was the same scene that Dad had carved at home but richer. The plaster figures were nearly life-sized, and all the people in the story were there. Mary and Joseph knelt in adoration, amazed at the miracle of the Nativity, and at their own part in it. Homely sheep nestled in the straw. Shepherds bowed shyly as the three kings marched grandly in at the door, bearing their gifts.

When I was small I could barely tear myself away from the crèche. I could have stood there all night, staring and dreaming. But Mom would draw me away into the church, my mittened hand small in her gloved one.

At first the church was dim, lit only by blazing, banked candles. On each side of the tabernacle on the altar, flowers massed darkly, and I could make out Christmas wreaths at the feet of the plaster saints—Patrick, Peter, and Teresa.

The organ hummed massively as we knelt, unbuttoning our coats. People crowded in and crowded in; the church filled up with coughs and scuffs and even whispers.

The deep organ hum burst into music as the lights came on. The dark clumps on the altar sprang into crimson life and were poinsettias. Father Quinlan in golden robes swept in from the vestry with four of the rough boys from the neighborhood. Gowned in white and red, solemnly carrying candles or incense, they were transformed. From rough, mean boys, they became angels. (This is a power of color and image. I never saw so much color so vividly as at Midnight Mass. Was that when the love of color and line seized hold of me, and my small fingers first itched to paint?)

Mass began. We prayed and sang, and heard the Christmas story read in grand and simple language: "She brought forth a son, her first-born, whom she wrapped in swaddling-clothes and laid in a manger, because there was no room for them at the inn."

Then, at last, came time for Communion. The crowd rose as one person and surged forward to the rail. Flanked by the four boys, Father Quinlan gave each of us in turn a share of God—a round wafer, white as snow, white as the holy purity we felt in our hearts.

Last Christmas Eve, when I thought of my folks going up to the rail together without me—Dad always went to Communion on Christmas Eve and Easter—I cried and hoped they missed me. This year it's much worse. I know now they are going separately to separate railings in separate churches. My world is entirely broken up. I hunger for that brittle round wafer, white as purity. Under the warm sleeping bag I shiver. Jason is warm, curled trustfully against me. I turn over and hug him.

December 25, Dawn

DREAM

A bright garden. Pure, quiet air. Flowers like jewels hide among grasses. A waterfall sings. Holy Pat, what can I be doing here? Never in my life have I walked in a garden like this one! Can I be dreaming?

I wander slowly toward the waterfall, careful not to crush the flowers in my path. Seeds brush against my long white gown. They cling a moment. Then they fall back to the rich earth. Yes, this is a dream.

I wake slowly, feeling entirely, foolishly, happy.

December 25, Noon

"Merry Christmas, Rianna!"

"And Happy Hanukkah to you. Don't give me that stuff
I'm a pagan."

"Yes, I know. But when you give a Christmas present,
you say Merry Christmas." I hold out the small, store-
wrapped parcel.

Rianna is sliding into her coat. Seeing the parcel, she
almost drops the coat. She smiles; she looks younger, my
age. "Sue! You got me a present! Hell, I haven't had a
present since I was a little kid!" Holding the gift, she looks
up at me, troubled. "I didn't get you one. I never thought."

Oh, the delight of it! The entire satisfaction of being the
thoughtful, loving one! I have given few presents in my life.
I hope in the future I can give more; this is fun!

"That's OK. You're a pagan. Look at you, you don't even
know you're supposed to open it."

Rianna lays her coat on the table. Carefully she unwraps
the herb-painted mug and lifts it in respectful hands.
"Awa!" Jason squawks in my arms, reaching for the pretty
thing.

"Oh, Sue, it's beautiful!"

"Just don't say it's what you've always wanted."

"But it is. I mean, if I'd seen it, I'd have wanted it, and
you knew that. But, Sue, you shouldn't have!"

I groan. "That's the other classic thing to say." It's true I shouldn't have, financially speaking. But Rianna's happy face is worth it. I'm surprised to find I don't regret the money.

"Where shall I put it?"

"The kitchen shelf is the usual spot, I think."

"But I want it extra safe, where I can see it. I'm going to admire it." In the end she leaves the mug by Isis, so "I'll see it first thing I come home. Right now we'd better go."

"We're fashionably late."

We're invited to Aunt Millie's for noon. Fussy, tidy Rianna is getting ready to walk out of here with her bed unmade and her orange-juice glass in the sink! She must have just got up. I guess you can sleep till noon if you don't have a small son to wake you up at the crack of every dawn. She gives her hair a hasty brush and adjusts her long green skirt and red shawl. For a pagan, Rianna really has the Christmas spirit!

"Let's not forget the wine," I remind her. Now there's an expense I do regret! But you can't very well turn up empty-handed for Christmas dinner.

"Um?" Jason asks, sitting heavy in my arms. "Um?"

"Bye-bye. We're going bye-bye to Aunt Millie's."

"All set?" Rianna whips into her coat and scarf and gloves. She picks up the wine. "Let's go!"

A bitter wind lashes State Street. The sky is as gray as the slush. Jason has on his red sweater and jacket, his best elephant-patch pants, and a cap that pulls down to his neck. But he still cries, "Awa!" when the wind bites him. I hug him tight, shielding him with my coat sleeves.

"What do you bet we get to sit in on the Santa Claus rite?" Rianna grumbles. "I always hated that bit."

"I loved it!"

"You must have gotten good presents."

"Not really. I loved the surprise." (And the expressed merry tenderness that filled the house along with the smell of roasting turkey.)

23

"Well, see, I was never surprised. I always got hankies, and then I had to jump up and down for joy. You know, Sue, that mug of yours is the best Christmas present I've ever had!"

I hug myself and Jason with delight. "Well, I bet we're too late for Santa Claus. They've opened their presents by now." Before dawn, probably.

"I hope! To tell the truth, I'm not looking forward much to dinner, either. Ghastly carbohydrates! Refined flour, sugar by the pound, and a bird that's been brutally murdered." My mouth waters. "Honest, Sue, Aunt Millie makes such a fuss about food! She's going to give herself heart trouble, eating like that all the time. I've told her so. It's not just Christmas, you know. They have potatoes every night."

We clump up the steps of 70 Main. There is a tarot card that perfectly represents 70 Main, even though the house on the card is a castle. Two girls hold up garlands—they seem to be dancing—and another huge garland nearly frames the card. I never draw that one; it means a happy home, Rianna has told me with a sigh.

Aunt Millie flings the door open. Huge and with wide-open arms, she wears a long silky red gown and slippers. Her gray hair is fuzzed. Her eyes—one blue, one brown—sparkle love at us. "Merry Christmas!" she cries, and falls on us like an avalanche, gathering the three of us to her soft bosom.

Rianna stiffens and draws away. Jason gurgles "Um-um!" and hurls himself into Aunt Millie's arms. She carries him triumphantly into the living room ahead of us. "We're all here," she shouts. "We can start!"

Before we can shrug off our coats, the room fills. Uncle Stan gets up from the couch and flicks off the TV. Kids rush in from the dining room and down the stairs, and we all converge on the Christmas tree by the window.

24

The tree is just a pile of glistening tinsel with cardboard Santas and Rudolphs stuck here and there, and a huge cardboard angel on top, crayoned by numbers. Nobody wastes a minute looking at it. The attraction is the pile of shiny wrapped packages beneath.

"Just what I feared," Rianna mumbles to me under cover of a fixed smile.

I understand that in California in the old days nobody asked anybody who they were or where they came from. Those were rude questions. So many people had gone West because of trouble with the law or their families, it was downright dangerous to poke around asking such questions. In the same way you don't ask Aunt Millie's foster kids who they are, or where they've come from. Their stories must be grim, often embarrassing, always sad.

Lisa comes last down the stairs, slow and dignified in a green dress, and high heels and stockings that are probably her first. Gold-brown hair bounces on her slender shoulders. She smiles shyly at us with eyes like Millie's, one blue, one brown.

The kids jostle and shout except for Anna. Anna hangs back, head down, hands clasped behind her. She's about ten, in a red and white brand-new dress and shiny patent leathers. Her kinky black hair is tied back with a red ribbon, but her dark face is sullen. Anna is new at Aunt Millie's.

Harry, thin and pale as he is, gets to the tree first. "Look, Susie," he says to me. "Jacie's got a present."

He points to a good-sized parcel in gold paper, marked JACIE in Millie's heavy round handwriting.

I am touched. Thank heaven we brought the wine! "Aunt Millie," I murmur, "Where shall we put this wine?"

But Millie doesn't hear. She's busy arranging us. "Young ones on the carpet. You're young, Carmen, that's right."

Carmen and Harry bounce up and down on the frayed

carpet. Anna sinks down behind them and curls herself small.

"Lisa, you hold Iggy. Here, on this chair."

Lisa sits daintily on a kitchen chair and accepts Little Eagle. Little Eagle is about Jason's age, but twice Jason's size. He looks around calmly from Lisa's lap, black eyes glowing in his brown face.

"Rianna, dear, you and Susie get the couch."

I hold out my arms for Jason, but Millie plumps him down in Little Eagle's playpen. I am amazed to see him stand there quietly, holding on to the bars. He sees me, but he doesn't cry or try to come to me.

Empty-armed, I lean back luxuriously on the dusty pillows. This freedom is itself a Christmas present! But Rianna nudges me, whispering "We're getting presents!" Following her gaze I notice two packages in the pile marked Susie and Rianna. I am embarrassed. But Rianna brightens. She smooths her long skirt and sits forward almost eagerly.

"We're ready," Millie calls, smacking her plump hands together. "Santa Claus, where are you? Calling Santa!"

"Hell!" Rianna whispers, and giggles.

We all look around for Santa. There's no Santa near the tree nor the card-heaped mantel nor the silent TV. (This must be the one moment of the year when it's turned off.)

"Santa Claus, appear!" Millie shrills.

The fake mistletoe dangling in the dining-room archway swings as Santa Claus bounds through into our midst. "Ho, ho, ho!" he booms hoarsely. "Are there any good kids here? These don't look very good to me!"

It's Uncle Stan, of course, in a plastic white beard and orange hunting jacket. Little Eagle's black eyes widen. Jay cries, "Um!" and reaches one hand toward Santa, clinging with the other to the playpen. Lisa blushes. I am sorry for

26

her. I bet her folks embarrass her a lot.

But Harry and Carmen are going wild. "We're good! We're good!" Carmen leaps about on her knees, brown eyes snapping. She wears crumpled jeans like mine with a floppy shirt, cut from the same cloth as Millie's gown. "So what if I'm bad!" she yells defiantly. "It's *Christmas*. So ho, ho, ho!"

"That's right," Santa agrees. "I almost forgot. Ho, ho, ho! And what have we here?" Stepping over Harry, he picks up the JACIE parcel. "Here we have Jacie. Who's Jacie? Never heard of him! Is he good?"

Clearly I hear Jason's "*Uuuum!*" over the uproar. "Ah, there's Jacie. He looks pretty good." Santa thrusts the parcel at Jason.

"Let me," I say, half rising.

But Millie is there first. She takes the parcel. "We don't want him eating the paper, Santa. Here, Harry, you open Jacie's present for him."

Harry walks over on his knees. Patiently he works at the package, murmuring to Jason, who keeps reaching through the bars.

"Come on, Harry," Carmen shouts. "We don't have all day!"

"Yes, we have, Carmen," Millie tells her softly. "We do so have all day."

Slowly Harry unties the ribbon and unfolds the paper. "Look, Jacie," he says, and holds up a little, plush brown bear with brown button eyes.

Jason stretches out both hands and plumps down on the playpen pillows. "Um!" he calls excitedly. "Dada, Dada!"

Next thing, he's hugging the bear, his small face glowing like the Christmas tree. I watch, amazed. And I had thought him too young to appreciate a present!

"He won't eat the eyes," Millie assures me. "They're put on with sail thread." But I wasn't worried about that yet.

2 7

I'm just hurting that I didn't think to give my son a bear—and glad that Millie did.

"OK, Santa, who's next?"

Santa growls, "Who's been good?"

"Oh, never mind about that. They've none of them been good!"

Harry and Carmen shout denials. Lisa hides her blushing face in Little Eagle's hair.

"OK, let's see. Whose is this one? Says *A-N-N-A*. Is there an Anna here?" Santa waves the package.

Anna looks up. Uncertainly, like in school, she raises a slow hand.

"Are you Anna, doll? Speak up."

Anna licks her lips. Very low, she mumbles, "Yes."

"Aaah, come on!" Carmen yells. "Open it!"

Santa leans across Carmen to hand Anna the package. To Carmen's disgust she opens it very slowly. As the paper flutters to the rug, she holds up a set of jackstones with a little red ball.

Rianna digs me in the ribs. This is the kind of present she used to get, just one notch better than hankies. With any kind of allowance Anna could buy herself a set of jackstones, holy Pat!

But wait. Anna's black eyes glow. Her lips part in a slow, unbelieving smile. She smiles around at all of us, silently showing us her treasure. Then she bends down like a praying Arab, drops a jack on the rug, and picks it up. Her pudgy hand is slow and awkward.

"OK," Millie calls. "What else you got, Santa?" She crashes onto the couch beside me, crushing me against Rianna. (I am overwhelmed with a sudden smell of sweat, powder, and strong perfume.) Lifting the hem of her gown, she rubs a large and swollen ankle.

"Ho, ho! How about *L-I-S-A?*"

Lisa sets Little Eagle down to open her present. He

clings to her knees, watching the rustling paper pop. Lisa holds up a white blouse printed with lavender leaves, with lace at the neck and wrists.

"Try it on," Millie urges. "Go on!" Lisa shakes her head.

"*I-G-G-Y!*" Santa roars. "Iggy, are you here?"

Little Eagle turns around to look at Santa. Carmen opens his present for him. Rocking on her knees, fairly jumping with impatience, she rips the package open. Little Eagle is too interested in the falling paper to notice his present—a set of wooden oblongs, sanded and brightly painted—till Carmen has built them into a tower.

Rianna digs at me again. This, too, is a pretty cheap gift; the blocks are scrap from Uncle Stan's shop. But they don't come from the shop sanded and painted!

Lisa's chair is empty. She has slipped away after all to try on her blouse.

Harry gets three new cars for a train set. Clasping the cars to his heart, he climbs over blocks and jackstones to whisper in Aunt Millie's ear. She hugs him hugely, smothering him entirely under one plump arm. Freed, Harry turns to the stairs.

"Hey, you!" Santa bellows. "Party isn't over!"

"Harry can't wait," Millie explains. "He's gotta run them. What's Christmas for, Santa?"

I ask, "Does he have trains upstairs?"

"All over his room and the bathroom. Santa, how about this nice girl here?"

"That nice girl, that's *S-U-S-I-E?*"

Rianna watches me closely as I open my gift. Embarrassed, I move as awkwardly as Anna, who is still dropping jacks and picking them up.

"I'll do it," Carmen offers, leaving the blocks to Little Eagle.

"You leave Susie alone!" Gently Millie pushes Carmen aside. "She's old enough to do her own."

2 9

Material lies folded in the bright paper. I lift and open it, and it unfolds into a large denim carry-all, with SUSIE appliquéd in red.

Exactly what I need for California! I peer inside. There's even a pocket where I can safely tuck my ticket. And I can turn it inside out, hide the SUSIE. There's room here for all my jeans, folded small.

"Aunt Millie," I stammer, "you, you, don't know how perfect this is!"

Millie twinkles at me. "It's for diapers, dear. And bottles. And Jacie's bear can fit in the pocket. And any other little stuff of your own, you know."

"Thanks so much!"

At this point, I see, Aunt Millie would like to be kissed. But everybody's watching, and Rianna's there on my other side, and Millie's own plump shoulder is in my way, and I'm not sure I want to kiss that flabby cheek. The moment passes.

"Santa," Millie calls, "there's a kid here going crazy!"

And Carmen finally gets her gift. In half a second it's open and scattered all across the rug. It's a magic kit, just what Carmen needs to entertain everybody. She claps on a plastic moustache and goes about challenging us to pick a card. "Pick a card, Anna! Susie, pick a card!"

Anna throws and retrieves jacks. Little Eagle murmurs to himself, feeling his blocks. Jason hugs Dada Bear and smiles like a cherub. Quietly Lisa comes back dressed in her new blouse and a blue skirt. She leans over the sofa and kisses her mother, as I wish I had done.

"That's so pretty, Lisa!" And it is. "Fits like a dream! I thought maybe I'd have to let out the seams, but it's perfect. Santa, I see one more present."

Rianna stiffens as Santa places the last package gently in her hands. She feels it, starts to shake it. "I wouldn't shake it, dear," Aunt Millie warns. So it's delicate.

"Rianna, pick a card! Want me to open that?"

Rianna shakes her head. Quickly, then, she opens the package. All of us except Anna, who is still throwing jackstones, lean to look. Rianna sits tautly, staring down at the gift in her lap.

"What is it?" Carmen wants to know. "What are they?"

They are a dozen long, tapered, night-black candles.

"I was never surprised," Rianna had said this morning about Christmas presents. Well, she's surprised now! In fact, she's shocked. She doesn't know how in the world to handle this present, what to say, or to whom. She just sits there like an ice statue.

Carmen touches the candles and keeps asking, "What are they?" Lisa leans over the couch, breathing down my neck, watching Rianna. Santa Claus peels off his beard and wipes his face with a red handkerchief. Even he looks troubled.

Millie explains. "They're for your religion, dear. I heard you used candles, too, like in church. They said especially black ones."

Rianna barely manages a soft "Thank you."

"What religion?" Carmen asks. "What's your religion, Rianna?"

Millie informs her calmly, "Rianna is a witch."

Lisa gasps. *"Really?"*

"Not really." Rianna sets the lid back on the candles and slides the whole package under the sofa. For safety? "Not the kind of witch you mean. I do believe in the Old Religion—that's true."

Still Carmen hovers. "But what's the candles for?"

Rianna lifts her head. Bravely she smooths the shielding hair away from her face. "Well, Carmen, I'll tell you. You bug me once too often, I'll light a black candle for you."

Carmen's face droops with disappointment. "Oh, I get it. Like Aunt Millie lit a candle for Lisa's math test."

"Not like that. I light this candle, and I call on my evil

familiar spirits." Rianna lifts dramatic hands. "I sing them my secret song—I mean, chant—and they come flying and find you and pinch you to pieces."

Carmen takes a step back and stumbles on Little Eagle's blocks. "You're kidding!"

Rianna smiles. "Are you sure?"

Uncle Stan stashes his red handkerchief in the pocket of his hunting jacket. "OK," he says loudly, "that's it. Santa wants a beer!"

Millie cries, "The turkey smells done!"

And it does. A beautiful smell fills the house, the rich smell of turkey and stuffing and onions and yams and hot breads and potatoes and squash and real coffee and three kinds of pie. Marvelous carbohydrates!

Aunt Millie struggles to get off the couch. I leap up and give her a hand. "Don't forget the wine, Aunt Millie."

But Rianna is already showing the wine to Uncle Stan. "Hey!" he cries happily. "Millie, look what the girls brought!"

"The turkey smells burned!" Millie wails, scuttling out through the archway.

Carmen steals a last awed glance at Rianna. Then she darts after Millie, shouting, "You said I can open the cranberry!"

"Awaaa!" Jason calls for the first time. "Zuzuzu!" He waves his bear at me. I pick them both up from the playpen.

Lisa lifts Little Eagle, unprotesting, away from his blocks. Everyone moves into the archway except Anna, who is throwing jackstones. Deaf to the cries of "Turkey!" and "A toast!" she throws jacks two, four, six, at a time and retrieves them. With each throw, her fingers move a little faster.

Hours later, altogether stuffed with carbohydrates,

3 2

Rianna and Jason and I take our leave. Dada Bear rides in my carryall, and Aunt Millie adds a package of leftover turkey on top of him. "Bless you, girls," she says at the door. "And, Susie, we'll all pray that next Christmas you and Jason will be back with your own family. How they must miss you!"

"Yes," I agree politely. "I miss them, too." There's no point in going into *that* matter. Millie thinks my family lives in New Mexico.

We bow into the bitter wind. Rianna's hair blows like banners, her skirt flies like a flag. "Well!" she exclaims, swallowing wind. "That was an ego trip for Aunt Millie!"

I am annoyed. I love Rianna. But why does she always see the dark side of everything and everyone? I once heard Uncle Stan remark that she was always "down at the mouth." Aunt Millie said yes, and she was worried that Rianna might go through life lonesome if she didn't learn how to smile. "It's disappointment did it," Millie added kindly. "She never had anyone to trust."

So I swallow my annoyance and speak quietly. "That was no ego trip. That was real." All that loving kindness! The way everyone got just what they wanted or needed— except Rianna, and even that was a darned good try. "Hey, you forgot your candles!"

I turn to go back. Rianna grabs my arm and hurries me forward. "Not exactly *forgot*. I'm not really the black candle-type witch, you know."

"You left them on purpose? Aunt Millie will be hurt!"

"Not till Easter. She won't clean under the couch till then."

I stop dead in the middle of a slush puddle. Jason kicks impatiently at my hip. "Awa! Awaaa!"

"Rianna," I say, bitter as the wind, "you're just jealous of Aunt Millie's goodness! Which is twice as real as your witchery!"

33

"Come on, Sue. It's too cold to argue here." We rush on into the wind.

Almost at the door of 114 State, Rianna says, "You know, you're right"—or I think that's what she says. She's mumbling into the wind, hiding her face in her coat collar, and maybe I hear her wrong.

Christmas Remembered

Our Christmas tree at home always stood by the living-room window. We did not throw the tinsel on with both hands and both feet. We hung it delicately, strand by strand. Birds flew in and out of the icicled branches. My Dad carved those birds before I was born, and Mom painted them to look like real winter birds. Chickadees swung upside down from the top branches. Pheasants strutted under the tree. The tinsel reflected red flashes where cardinals flew.

Brightly wrapped presents were piled under the tree by the crèche. Mom always gave us her knitting—mittens and caps, sweaters and socks. I might give her a compact, and my Dad a paperback about big game. Dad gave weird presents. One Christmas he gave me a fishing pole I never thought of using. Another time I got a mitt. I traded that for a makeup kit at school, and Mom found out. Holy Pat! I was in the fourth grade then.

We had a color TV in the corner. Evenings its purple light played over the tree and the birds and the crèche. Out in the warm kitchen Mom would be rolling ginger cookies; the whole house would smell spicy. In the front hall a candle burned before the picture of the Sacred Heart. When I think of home now—and I try not to—I think of the tarot card with the dancing girls and garlands. It really was a happy home.

Things Remembered

FALL, TWO YEARS AGO

How did I come this far into the cold country of the Queen of Swords? Why are Jason and I alone together at Christmastime?

In the beginning it was Mom's fault.

Mom saw in the Springerton *Mirror* that the Civic Center was going to show art works by young people, aged fifteen to twenty. "Why don't you try?" she suggested. "Jack never tries; Jack never does. And that goes for Jill, too."

"Oh, I'm not that good," I said.

"You won the art prize last year. You must be good!"

"That was just at Holy Name, Mom. These people will be from all over Springerton and Mechanicsville."

"I bet you're as good as any of them! Go ahead, Susan; reach for a star. It's an ill wind that blows no one good."

"What? What ill wind, Mom?"

"Why, the mess! All these months your room's been looking like an art store; we might as well get some good out of it."

I tried to keep my room tidy, but I had such a lot of stuff: watercolors, pastels, broken stubs rolling around the floor; the big easel Dad made me, and the little old one Maureen gave me; stacked paintings, rolled drawings, and a full waste basket. Mom never complained about it, but I saw what she meant; here was a chance to make it all worthwhile.

36

Mom kept urging, and I myself wanted to try; I wanted to see how I matched up. Just suppose Mom was right, and I really was as good as any of them. Wouldn't that be great to know? And as my friend Maureen said, "What have you got to lose?"

On a golden fall Saturday I took the bus into Springerton, hugging my portfolio. It had flowers painted on it, and SUZANNE lettered across the top. I thought that looked more sophisticated than Susan.

I felt altogether sophisticated that morning! I had on my best blue linen-look skirt and silky blouse. Full brown curls—with bronze highlights from Maureen's bottle—bounced on my shoulders. And on top of all that, I was slender. But I didn't even think about that; I took it for granted.

I took it for granted! I hadn't a notion in the world what a dose of real life could do to a person's figure and good looks—or that real life would actually come up to me that day and take me by the hand. I jiggled around on that bus seat, clutching my portfolio, while Mechanicsville turned into Springerton, feeling adventurous. If I had drawn a tarot card then, it would have been the Knight of Swords, galloping into battle with ferocious joy. That was me. I cringe now, remembering my innocence.

At the Civic Center I joined a milling crowd of all types of teen-age artists. They carried portfolios and statues in paper bags, and rolled-up watercolors, and knitting bags with bright stitchery peeping out, and enormous oils in frames. I expected to find a real artist in charge, and I was very interested to meet him. I had never met a real artist—Sister Teresa didn't count—and I hoped for an earnest, bearded young man with deepset eyes.

The bald man I found giving orders was a businessman. He wore a gray suit and polished shoes and had a paunch. "Find your own spot," he told me hurriedly. "Hang your

37

own stuff. There's equipment on Table C if you need it."

One long wide hall was the art show. Kids were taping pictures to the walls, hanging canvases, setting clay heads on shelves. Anybody could show anything; there was no test you had to pass.

I was a bit disappointed. I had hoped to pass a test. In my flowered portfolio I carried the portrait of Mom with her back turned and a watercolor of Maureen. I was big on watercolor and pastel that year. I loved delicate colors and intricate drawing. Later—when my life turned heavy—I went in more for oil.

I started to put these up next to a bunch of huge glossy photos of public buildings that a very handsome young man was hanging. Glancing sideways at him, I noticed he had short, dark curls and dark eyes. He wore expensive-looking jeans with a cashmere turtleneck and fancy boots. And he was eyeing me with . . . admiration! Feeling confused and shy, I stepped quickly back to see if Maureen's portrait hung straight.

Seeing my two pictures alongside other people's gave me a shock. I had thought mine pretty good, but beside the others, they were amateur stuff. The others were much richer in detail, subtler in color. I went forward to rip mine down.

The young man stopped me. He actually grabbed my hands and held them! He said, "Hold on now. Your stuff isn't bad. It's pretty good, considering."

No young man, even the homeliest, had ever touched me before. This dreamy character held on to my hands firmly, his dark eyes smiled down at me. My heart thundered.

"Considering what?" I asked boldly.

"Considering you're only a high school senior."

"Sophomore."

"I don't believe it! You're at least eighteen."

"Sixteen."

38

Paul laughed. He folded our fingers together and swung our hands lightly back and forth. "Why admit it?" he teased. "I would never have guessed!"

Paul persuaded me to leave my pictures up. Politely I admired his photos. He had hung twenty of them, but the paunchy businessman suggested he take half of them down. "Leave some room for somebody else."

I helped him choose the ten to take down and to rearrange the winners.

"You'd think they'd want some *good* stuff in here," he murmured. "But that's the trouble with a nonjury show. How about some lunch, ah"—he glanced quickly down at my labelled portfolio—"Suzanne? You like spaghetti?"

Paul was easy to get to know; he talked freely. Over spaghetti and salad, he told me he was already a professional photographer and just going to college for the degree. Over coffee, he said he meant to work for some big magazine, travel all over the world. Over dessert, he said, "In half an hour I'm going to see a great show with famous camera angles. Want to come?"

"What time is it?"

"Four."

Four o'clock? Holy Pat! Mom would soon be looking for me.

"Call home," Paul suggested.

Call home and say what? That I had met a beautiful young man who liked me? I could hear Mom's answer to that! "Get yourself on that bus, young lady! I'll expect you in half an hour."

"Say you met a girl friend," Paul advised lightly.

Deep inside me, Sister Teresa's voice whispered, "Satan is the father of lies." I hesitated maybe a full minute. Paul watched me with kind, laughing eyes. "Suzanne," he said, "you look like a Renoir. Has anyone told you that?"

39

I called home. Mom's hello sounded a bit anxious. "Mom," I said, "Everything's OK. I hung the pictures—"

"They accepted them for the show?"

"Oh, yes."

"I told you so! I told you, you were as good as any of them!" Mom laughed with delight.

"Mom, I met a . . . girl here. She's a friend of Maureen's. I think she's a cousin." Maureen was in New Hampshire at a funeral; Mom couldn't ask her. And why should she ask anyhow? I had never lied to her before. "And we thought we'd take in a movie. OK?"

December 27, Afternoon

All the way out Federal on the bus I've been half expecting to go home. I nearly got off at Jackson. I did peer down the street and see the second house on the right. It's gray now instead of red, and there are two VWs parked in the driveway instead of Dad's pickup.

Jason is getting restless. He starts in, "Awa, awa!" And people turn around and stare at us.

I look hopefully out the window. Houses I know jog past. They're big houses, two family; Dad used to say there was a lot of money tied up in them. But in this cold gray light they look downright dismal, in spite of their red-bowed wreaths and plastic Santas. If I ever have money to tie up, I won't tie it up in a house on Federal, or on Mayberry or Tyler or Margery. I'll buy a beach cabin in California.

Oak Street is next. I button Jason's jacket and draw his cap down over his ears and pull the buzzer. Just in time. He was getting set to start yelling. Now the strangeness shuts him up.

The houses with money tied up in them end on Margery. Oak Street is just two notches better than State. 60½ Oak is gray clapboard, chipped, with broken steps. Just looking at it, I feel my heart sink. I had been hoping Dad could help me out with money, at least, but this doesn't look like it. This looks as if Dad has "come down in the world," as Mom would say.

I set Jason down on the broken top step. He is silent, looking about in wonderment. Holding his hand, I knock.

A plastic curtain tweaks in the window. I hear footsteps coming to the door, and my throat lumps up. I know those footsteps so well! They creaked past my door every morning just before the alarm rang. They thumped up the porch steps every night at six; and Mom would put her knitting down and go in the kitchen to mash potatoes.

The door opens. Before I can see him clear, Dad is hugging me. His arms are tight and strong; his chin is bristly against my cheek. He smells of pipe tobacco, like always. I will not cry! I hug him back. Jason whimpers because I have let go of his hand, and hangs onto my leg. Dad and I hug and hug. We sway and gasp together till Dad chuckles, "Next door they'll think I've got a new girl friend. Come on in, Suki."

He lets me go and steps back. We follow him into the kitchen. Our old round table is there, covered with Sunday papers and *Field and Stream*. Dad's pipe sits in a full ashtray; his boots lean together on the brown rug Mom braided. The kitchen cupboards are half built; stock for them leans in a corner with a keg of nails. So far it looks like home, with Mom week-ending at her sister's. But I miss the clean oil-and-ginger smell of Mom's kitchen.

Dad himself has changed. Now I see him, he looks thinner than before, and somehow younger. He's a downright handsome man, except for his shabby work pants, sweat shirt, and slippers. Tears stand in his blue eyes. He says, "Suki, I thought I'd lost you!"

Jason clutches my jeans. "Zuzu?"

Dad stoops to him, holding out a calloused hand. Jason stares up at Dad, and plunks his thumb in his mouth.

I lift him up so they'll be more eye to eye. "Dad, this is Jason."

Jason squirms around and hides his face on my shoulder.

42

Dad smiles, but his eyes are sad. He says "I wish your mother was here to see him! Sit you down, Suki."

I ease down onto one of the kitchen chairs. It wobbles. I try to put Jason down, but he won't go. He clings and sucks his thumb. He won't let me take off his coat, and he won't move so I can take mine off. We perch there as if we're ready to spring up and fly away.

Dad turns to the stove. "You drink coffee?"

"Of course!"

I startle myself, sounding cross. When I left home, I had just begun to drink coffee, and Mom was fussing about it. If he had asked me then, that's how I would have answered, "Of course!" crossly. It's as though we had never been apart, though heaven knows I feel apart! The handsome, shabby man pouring coffee over there is my Dad, and yet he isn't. He is a younger man who lives in a different house. I don't know where his bathroom is or who his friends are now. He doesn't know my son.

Mildly he says, "I guess I should have asked, *How* do you drink coffee?"

"With sugar and milk, please."

"What I thought."

Dad brings two steaming plastic cups to the table. He sits in the other chair, next to *Field and Stream*. He reaches out a hand to me, and I take it. Holding hands quietly, we blow our coffee cool. Jason steals a look at Dad. When he sees Dad watching, he hides his face again.

"I guess you want to know about your mother."

"Tell me."

"You know she only stayed with me because of you." I never dreamed of such a thing! "We didn't get on real well for years, not since before you started school. It was my fault, I guess. You know I couldn't keep away from the skirts."

Yes. I am not altogether confounded, so I must have

43

known it. The knowledge lived like a bogieman in a dark room in my mind, and I just never looked in there. "I couldn't help it, and she couldn't stand it. That's how it was." And you were Catholic and couldn't get divorced.

"There was more to it. You can guess." I can? To do that, I would have to stand away back from my folks and see them as real people, like Paul and me. I never thought of them like that; they were always the grown-ups, the ones in charge. They ran my world, and I never dreamed they might not run their own. Dad's talk is turning on lights in more dark rooms in my mind.

"We went on like that for I don't know how long. I'd go out nights, come in late; she wouldn't scold. She didn't want you to hear. But, you remember, she moved over to the spare room."

Yes. I helped her. I carried drawers full of sacheted undies across the hall to the little sewing room, not much bigger than a closet. "Your father *snores* so," she explained. Holy Pat, I knew that was true! Saturday mornings his snore shook the house. I never thought anymore about it. I never wondered, either, why Dad never went to Mass except on Christmas and Easter. I just figured he wasn't as religious as other kids' fathers.

"I kept thinking about separating, but she wouldn't hear of that. She said you needed a home with both parents in it. And she was right, you know." Yes, I do know! "When you have a kid, the kid comes first. It isn't just what *you* want anymore; it's what's right for the kid. You know that yourself.

"We did all right. Once we made the rules, we got along. It wasn't much of a marriage—you know what I mean. It was a nice home though. I miss it."

Dad pulls his hand gently out of mine to light his pipe.

I miss it, too! I have missed it ever since I left. Under the bravado I have always been homesick. On a gray, cold day

44

like this, I used to come home from school, and the warmth would wrap itself around me. There'd be milk and cookies on the kitchen table, and a chicken in the oven, and lights on to chase away the grayness. Later, when I went to bed, I might hear the folks talking downstairs, or Mom would have the radio crooning in the kitchen while she washed up. And I would fall asleep with safety warmer than a blanket around me.

Dad takes my hand again. "And, of course, there was the money problem. I spent a bit on skirts, I admit. And I didn't always end up at the shop mornings." Though he always left the house at six thirty, dinner pail in hand.

"I didn't know about the money." We always seemed to have enough.

"Well, your mother wouldn't likely talk to you about that." She was great at secrets, that's for sure!

"Then, when you . . . blew up in her face . . . things went altogether to pieces. She quit cleaning house. No point to it. Next thing she went and got herself a job."

Mom? A job? "What job?"

"Taking ads at the *Springerton Mirror*. We had frozen dinners every night, would you believe!" It's not easy to, Mom was always a proud cook. "She lost weight. She never had much, you know. Well, before we were through, she could have modeled bikinis." Dad sighs and puffs on his pipe.

"And then?"

"And then she started coming home late. *I* was waiting up for *her*. It was enough to send a man back to Ireland! Then one night she just didn't come home at all."

Jason wriggles. He pulls his thumb out of his mouth and slides down me to the floor. "Just don't let him in the corner," Dad says. "I don't want him in my nails. Bright kid, ain't he!"

"She didn't come home. So what did you do?"

"Nothing." Dad puffs calmly.

"Nothing! You didn't call the—the missing persons' people?"

"Holy Pat, what for! I knew nothing had happened to her; she was all right. She just didn't want to come home. Nothing there for her. I did call the *Mirror*, but she'd left there, too. Hey, look at your kid!"

That didn't take long! As if he had understood Dad's words, Jason has crawled straight for the nails. Now he's picking nails out of the keg, looking at them, and dropping them. In a minute he'll eat one. I rush over and grab him.

For the first time in this house Jason speaks, "Awa!"

And under his "Awa!" I hear another sound—a soft creak, from away beyond the kitchen door, like when someone gets up off an old couch as quietly as they can.

"Dad!" I whisper.

But Dad is looking with interest at Jason's cross face. "You know, Suki, he looks like her—your mother!"

"Dad, *pssst!*" He turns to me. I nod excitedly toward the door. Someone beyond the door sighs and shuffles.

"That's Glory," Dad says calmly. "She's been asleep." He calls out, "Glory, come meet my Suki!"

A husky voice answers, "OK."

Clutching Jason hard against me, I face the door. In slinks a very thin blonde woman and sags in the doorway. Her face is papery, smudged with stale makeup. Her hair straggles down bowed shoulders. She wears a pink shiny dressing gown and pink, pointed slippers. "Hi, Suki," she says, looking away from me.

"I mean Susan." Dad corrects himself. "My daughter, Susan."

Glory nods to me. "Who's the kid?"

"And this is Jason," Dad says proudly. "My grandson."

"Kitchie-coo!" says Glory. "Cute kid!" Jason stares at

46

her. His thumb dives back in his mouth. "I gotta get dressed," she tells Dad.

"You going in?"

"I told you, I go in for five, Sundays. Pleased to meet you," she tells me. She smiles a thin smile at Jason and steals away.

Still clutching Jason, I sink down onto my shaky chair. Jason is quiet now. He sucks his thumb steadily. Dad puffs, not looking at me.

When I get my breath back, I ask, "Where . . . does Glory . . . work?"

"Appledore Inn. She waits on tables." I remember the Appledore. The Children of Mary had Communion breakfasts there. The waitresses stole around in blue-and-white uniforms and nurse's shoes.

I am suddenly altogether restless. The place was shabby before; now it's ugly! I don't want to stay here five minutes more. I don't want to see Glory again—that's for sure—or have her overhearing our talk anymore. I can't look at Dad. He doesn't look at me. I say, "I think we'd better go."

"But you just came!"

"I know, but . . . you don't have a playpen, do you?"

"No. But—"

"Where can I put Jason? I'd have to chase him the whole time, or he'd eat your nails." And God knows what else. "He's lively."

"Yes, I see that."

"And I forgot his bottle."

That settles it. Dad reaches over the table and takes Jason's little hand in his fingers before Jason sees him coming. Jason freezes against me. I hate to see them like this. They're relatives. They should live next door to each other. Dad should baby-sit with Jason on Saturdays; Jason should know him like his own father. . . .

"He's a grand kid, Suki." Dad lets the small hand go. "How are you fixed for money?"

"Not too good. But neither are you." I'm not asking for anything!

"Welfare?"

"Right."

"Sometimes you can do better like that than working!" I'd rather work any day—someplace they don't allow babies, like maybe a bar. Dad feels in his shirt pocket. "I've got you a little Christmas present." He pulls out a sealed envelope and pushes it across to me. "Not as much as I'd like it to be, but. . . . You got plans?"

Mumbling thanks, I slip the envelope into my pocket. Briefly I explain about California. His face lights up at the word. "Somewhere I've always wanted to go—California! Pick oranges in winter. Seems like the older I get, the more I mind the cold. But give me your address there, so I don't lose you again."

I jot the address down on *Field and Stream.* Dad turns it around and inspects it. "South Beach Design. Isn't that the art school you were thinking of . . . before?"

"Yes, it is. I won a scholarship."

Dad marvels. "You must be really good! But, Suki, do you still think there's money in art?"

"Not fine art, Dad, commercial art—like for ads."

"Yeah?" He puffs thoughtfully. "I guess someone gets paid for those."

"Dad, can you think of any place I could . . . leave . . . Jason for a couple of years? I don't want to take him to South Beach Design." I don't say I *can't* take him because that wouldn't be fair. I see now that Dad can't carry any part of my cross; he's got his own.

"You think that's a good idea? Leave the kid?"

"No, it's not a good idea, but it's . . . necessary."

"Rough on a little kid." What he means is, "Just what

your mother did not do to you."

"Yes, I know."

"If your mother was here. . . . Of course, there's the Holy Infant over in Springerton."

I shake my head firmly. I used to love nuns. When I was ten I planned to be one, but now I'm an outsider. Dad said I "blew up in Mom's face"; well, I blew up in the nuns' faces, too; and I took their bag of tricks and goodies and threw it so far away that there's no finding it. Now if I see a nun coming, I get out of the way.

Dad nods. "OK. Then there's Family Service. They're not religious or anything."

Rianna has told me about Family Service. She grew up in some foster homes that were pretty bad—nothing like Aunt Millie's. I don't too much like the idea, but time is short. "That's a good thought."

"See them Monday, Suki. Red tape takes time. But if I was you, I'd think it over pretty carefully. If only your mother was here. . . ."

Dad doesn't need to harp on Mom. I know perfectly well it's against all the rules to go off and leave a little kid—he needn't remind me. But what ever happened to all the rules, anyhow? If God wrote them, as I used to think, He sure hasn't been enforcing them!

Amazingly clear, a memory flashes.

The summer I was seven, I was sitting on our front steps waiting for Maureen to come over when Arthur Harrison from down the street came by slowly, head down, scuffing his sneakers. Arthur always had marbles on him, and because Maureen was late, I called to him to have a game.

Arthur shrugged. We played, and I won! Arthur played badly, which was not too surprising, seeing as big tears kept streaking his face. Finally I asked what was wrong.

"Nothin'," he said, swiping a tear with the back of his

hand. "Nothin', but my Dad's getting married is all."

I felt wise. "He is not, Arthur. Your Dad's already mar-ried."

"Not anymore. He's divorced. He's gonna marry Aunt Betty—"

"He is not! He can't marry his sister." I knew the rules.

Arthur explained quite patiently. "She isn't his sister. She's Mrs. Snark. I'm supposed to call her Aunt Betty is all."

"Well, then, if she's a *Mrs.*, she's married already!"

"Not anymore. She's divorced. She's going to marry my Dad and come live at our house, and so are all her kids, is all."

This was frightening news! Married people could get divorced—that meant unmarried—and then get married again? You could break up a family and start a new one? Suppose you didn't like your new family!

I ran indoors, yelling, *"Mom-ee! Mom-ee!"*

Mom was ironing clean sheets that smelled of sunshine. "Help me fold," she said.

We stood apart and shook the sheets between us and folded them, coming together. Mom's words calmed me. "We are Catholics," she explained. "When we get married, it's forever." My family could never break up like the Harrison's.

It was as simple as that. My world was safely run by Catholic rules. So long as we all kept those rules, we were all safe. . . .

Glory comes back into the room. She stands straight now; her makeup is fresh; her hair shines golden. She wears the trim blue-and-white uniform of the Appledore Inn. Her ruffled cap is stuck in her coat pocket, and her thin legs in high-heeled boots.

She speaks directly to me, "You take the bus on Federal?"

"Yes."

"So do I. Let's go together."

I stand up. Holding Jason on my hip, I lean over Dad and kiss his hard cheek that smells of tobacco. "Thanks for the money," I whisper. "Thanks for everything."

There is much too much to say, and just no way at all to say it. A good thing entirely Glory's there! If we were alone, I might try to say some of it and get mixed up and cry and sit down and never go.

Dad holds me hard. "Let me know where you are, from now on."

"Oh, I will. And if Mom . . . you let me know. . . ."

"Holy Pat, what do you think? And, Suki, I'm sorry."

So am I! O God, am I sorry. I'm sorry I hurt Dad and pulled the rug out from under Mom, and blew up in her face. If only I had listened to them, we would be together now. I wouldn't be kissing Dad again and pulling away and going off to California. Mom would never have left. Jason would be their real grandson. Except that I wouldn't have Jason at all! And Mom really wanted to leave, all the time. What would Sister Teresa say, "God works in mysterious ways"? I am grief-torn, confused altogether.

"I'm awfully sorry, Dad." I pull away. Leaving him, I suddenly see why he looks younger. I remember his hair all gray. Now it's only gray in front. He's got one gray curl hiding the lines on his forehead, and all the rest is brown.

Going up toward Federal, Jason toddles between Glory and me, holding both our hands. He looks up at Glory with interest and no fear. He seems to like her.

She says, "Your daddy's a sweet man."

51

"Yes." I am uneasy. I don't know how to look at Glory, let alone talk to her!

Maybe she senses this. She says, "I just met him last summer."

"Oh." That does help quite a bit. She wasn't one of the skirts he chased while Mom waited up.

"Never knew such a sweet man. He'd give you his last crust—not his last tobacco, mind, but his last crust—if you needed it. Bet he was a good daddy, huh?"

"Yes." And now I am remembering how good. I'm remembering little gifts—ribbons, candy, rubber balls— what he called "unbirthday presents." I'm remembering the easy puzzles we worked together on winter Saturdays, when he would rather have watched football. His arms were strong around me when I came home crying, scared of the rough boys. And he was the one who went to see Sister Teresa about my math.

"Look," says Glory, "he's so happy he's found you. Don't lose him again! You know that night you called up? He cried that night he was so happy. He couldn't have been happier if. . . . Look, now you're grown-up; maybe you can help him."

Me, help Dad? "How?"

"Just be there. He gets awful lonesome, Suki—Susan. Lonesome for his family, like a homesick kid."

So when I go to California on January sixth, I'll be leaving two homesick kids behind me—Jason and Dad. Holy Pat, that makes me feel great!

But I'm surprised. I like Glory; Glory is a nice woman.

December 27, Evening

"Sounds like a bitch to me," says Rianna. "Knew you were coming, didn't she? No playpen, no lunch—you think that was an accident? Sure she was nice—when you were leaving! How much did he give you anyhow?"

"Fifty bucks."

"Well, that's great! That'll get you to Chicago."

"It really was great, Rianna. He didn't exactly have it lying around loose."

"OK, OK—it's the thought that counts. Thing is, where do you go from here?"

"That's what I don't know!" I say, nearly crying.

I am tired; we had a long ride back on the bus, and Jason squalled the whole way—I really had forgotten his bottle—and I've a cold hollow inside me. Times like this, I wonder what I would ever do without Rianna. If I still said prayers, I would thank God every night that Jason once got howling sick and Rianna came to our rescue. Otherwise, we might never have met. Jason and I would still be entirely alone, and tonight I would be lugging him up the cold stairs to our mattress, both of us crying all the way. Rianna's got one big fault—that cynical bitterness that keeps everybody but me at ten-foot-pole distance. It doesn't bother me; I understand it—usually.

Now Rianna's rustling up dinner while I set out the plastic dishes and the new Christmas mug. She's frying soybeans with brown rice, and there's lettuce for dessert. Healthy, no doubt, but I say, "I've got a can of lasagna upstairs. Want me to get it?"

Rianna snorts. "Canned glop? Hell, no! But go get the kid's bottle."

Jason had fallen asleep, entirely exhausted, on her bed. But now he's stirring, making miserable noises. I dash upstairs and heat his aba. And, while it heats, I gulp down a cold can of macaroni and cheese; it calms my nervous stomach.

By this time, I can hear Jason roaring downstairs. I wrap the aba in a mitten—it's too hot—and race back. Rianna has made no attempt to calm him. I change and soothe him and cool off the hot aba under the faucet while she dishes up the soy-rice mess.

As we eat, Rianna says, "I've been thinking. You could talk to Aunt Millie."

"No!" There is no reason on God's earth why that overworked, overgood woman should take on my son! I may be selfish—every blade of grass has to be selfish enough to fight for its share of sun—but I have some pride left, some sense of right and wrong. "No, I won't."

"OK. I respect your scruples. That leaves Elaine."

"Elaine!" A lump of rice-soy actually cools on my fork as I take this in. "Elaine Richards? Paul's mother?"

Rianna nods calmly, picking up her mug. "She's the kid's grandmother, isn't she?"

I call from Ahmed's. This time I go well-armed with change, pad, and pencil. When Info gives me the number I write it down, and then I keep the pencil handy to jot down directions, times, whatever Elaine cares to tell me.

The phone rings once and is quietly picked up. "Good evening," says the cool voice I remember, "Richards's residence."

"Ah, ah, hello. Mrs. Richards?"

"Speaking."

"Ah, Mrs. Richards, this is Susan." No response. No gasp, nothing. Elaine breathes gently, waiting. "You know, Susan O'Hara, Paul's friend—Suzanne."

"Oh, yes. Yes, of course. How are you, Suzanne?" Her voice brightens as though she's glad it's me. This is called poise, or *savoir faire*.

"Fine. I mean, Mrs. Richards, did you know we had a baby Paul and me his name's Jason he's a year old?"

A silence follows. I wait for the operator to interrupt. Then slowly, "Are you sure?"

"Oh, yes, I'm sure. He looks just like Paul. Mrs. Richards, would you like to see him?"

"I—I—" Elaine is off balance. "Yes, I would. And I'd like to see you too, Suzanne."

"When can we come?"

Here the operator breaks in. I feed the phone.

"Suzanne? Are you there?"

"Oh, yes."

"I'll be free to see you,"—I can almost see her consulting the calendar—"I'll be free Saturday, January second. Is that convenient?"

"Oh, yes!" Never mind, convenient; I'd walk out there through snow and wolves in the small hours if she'd see me!

"Could you come to tea at four o'clock?"

"Oh, yes!" I am hugging myself.

"Do you have a car?"

"Oh, no. We'll take the bus."

"I'm afraid no bus comes this far out. Have you a driver's license?"

"Oh, yes!" Though I haven't touched a steering wheel since Paul left.

"Rent a car. I will reimburse you."

"Oh! Thank you very—"

55

"Naturally I want very much to see Joseph."

"Jason." She keeps saying "I." What about Mr Richards?

"January second then. I'll be looking forward to it."

"Oh, me, too! Thank you!"

A soft, deliberate *click*. Right away I jot down "Jan. 2, 4:00." I hope I remember the way.

Things Remembered

FALL, TWO YEARS AGO

On that cloudy November Saturday a bitter wind whipped Main Street. Paul and I trotted along, holding hands, letting the wind push us. I hung back to look at a store window full of dresses.

"You'll freeze solid, standing here," Paul said. "I bet you'd like to stand here all day!"

"I could look at just that one all day." I pointed to an ankle-length sheath of shimmering gold stuff.

"Well, meantime you're turning purple." Paul took off his big camel's-hair coat and threw it over both of us like a tent. We huddled together under it, and his arm hooked around my waist. He laughed and poked fun at the dresses.

The wind and the crowds rushed past behind us. We shivered and laughed together, and the bright dresses glowed behind the glass like flowers in a greenhouse. Paul's warmth and his arm pressing me blocked out everything else. Even while I pointed and giggled—to hear his soft laugh in my ear—I hardly saw the dresses. I forgot the cold altogether.

"Come see over here."

Paul drew me on to the next window which was less colorful: just shoes and gloves and—"Oh!"

"What?" Paul was instantly alert.

"Nothing. Nothing!" I had seen the price tag.

"Let me guess." Paul's dark gaze flicked quickly around

the window. "It's not the brogues or the scarf. Aha!" He pulled away from me. "You wait here; I'll be right back."

Leaving me standing there draped in his coat, he darted into the store. A minute later I saw him with a clerk in the inside of the window. He pointed right at It, and shot me a questioning look. I smiled. He had guessed right. It was a brown leather handbag with zippers and clasps and compartments for lipstick and files and eyeshadow and powder and combs and keys and bills and change and tickets and pens, and room enough for a small sketch pad.

The clerk lifted It out of the window. He and Paul disappeared in the dimness of the store.

Startled out of my foolish dreamy state, I ran inside. "Paul, don't; you mustn't—"

He was pulling bills out of his wallet. Rushing up, I glimpsed a lot more left within. "Suzanne," he said sternly, "don't make a scene. We're in public."

So I didn't make a scene. I stood and watched the clerk wrap It in a bag, while Paul stuffed change into his pocket. Astonished thoughts raced through my head: It's so beautiful, but I never meant to hint. He must like me. Holy Pat, Paul must really like me!

My heart filled with grateful tenderness. "Paul," I said, "put your coat on. I do have mine, you know."

"Actually, that's not a bad idea." Paul handed me the bag of It and eased his coat over his athletic shoulders. A minute later we were trotting again before the wind, hand in hand.

That was Paul—warm, generous, impulsive—rich. He lived an independent life of amazing freedom. I had long noticed that people in movies or on TV never seemed to have any folks. Everyone I knew had them. But nobody in a movie ever called home and said, "Mom, I'm going to be late. . . ." Paul was like someone in a movie. He never mentioned his folks; at that point I wasn't sure he had any. He lived entirely on his own.

Even more surprising than this physical freedom was his complete mental freedom. I began to see my own thinking as "indoor" thinking. My thoughts were safely confined inside four mental walls.

For instance, every Sunday I went to Mass. "Why?" Paul asked, and I couldn't really explain. That was what one did on Sundays.

Dinner was at six thirty, and I must not be late. "Grab a sandwich," said Paul. "Skip dinner." Skip dinner? Then what would I do at six thirty?

I worked awfully hard at algebra, which I hated. "Why the hell?" Paul asked. "You'll never use algebra in your life!"

"But marks are important." As everyone knew!

"Why?"

"Well . . . if you do something, you're supposed to do it as well as you can." Everyone knew that, too.

"Why? I mean yes, if it's something that matters to you—like art matters to you. But why worry with algebra?"

And I just couldn't say why.

That was the way we talked. Paul opened mental doors, and I walked through them . . . hesitantly.

Now scurrying down Main Street before the wind, Paul said, "I hear this movie isn't all that good. Let's go to my place instead."

"Oh!" I was shocked entirely. "But I can't do that!"

Instantly he asked, as I knew he would, "Why?"

"Well, people don't. I mean, girls don't." At least, not girls from Holy Name.

59

Paul laughed, and I saw that this, too, was indoor thinking. I had always simply accepted these four mental walls. Now I stood inside them, and Paul stood outside in the free air and laughed at me. If I stuck indoors too long, he might walk off and leave me there. He said, "Suzanne, I *dare* you to come see my place!"

I darted a quick glance at his handsome happy face. I was panting, running to keep up with him. Breathless, I squeezed his hand.

"Good. It's just around here."

We darted around the corner onto Sunfield Street, where all the fancy apartments were. Paul's building was Number 10, second on the left.

We burst into a lobby with carpets and mailboxes and an elevator. Paul hustled me into the elevator, but not before I caught the amused look on the doorman's face.

We held hands all the way up in the elevator. My heart was thumping as if I was going on a safari, not just visiting a friend's apartment. I felt altogether brave. On the top floor, he let me into his living room.

I'm not sure why it surprised me so much, maybe just because it was so neat, as if Mom had just cleaned it. The sofa and two easy chairs were green-upholstered, and the carpet was green. The curtains were printed white and green, a geometric pattern. "It came furnished," Paul reminded me. At one end of the room was the kitchen alcove, and at the other end a small bedroom. I looked quickly away from the bedroom, though the wide bed was made, and no clothes lay piled about. As I said, Mom might just have cleaned it.

Paul went to the two front windows and drew down the shades. "What are you doing?" I asked nervously.

"Atmosphere. I'm very sensitive to atmosphere, Suzanne. Now all we need is—" He punched a knob, and sound flooded the room. It was music, but enormous, overpowering music. It sent chills up my spine. "Beethoven," Paul told me reverently.

"Could—could it be softer?"

"Sure. Beethoven can be overpowering." Paul gentled the music. Then he came to me.

In the near dark, in the powerful music, in Paul's arms, I nearly lost myself. I went all soft, and someone inside me cried silently Yes! Yes! Yes! My arms were stealing around Paul's neck when something dropped *thud* on the floor beside me.

I came to. My new handbag, Paul's gift, had fallen and waked me. Just in time I leaped out of Paul's arms. I rushed to the window and zoomed the shade up. Cold light flooded the room with daylight sense. Trembling, I made myself breathe again. "That was almost sin," I told myself. "And besides, it's dangerous. You can get in bad trouble like that."

To Paul I said faintly, "It's getting late."

He stood quietly, smiling. "Is it?"

"I'd better go."

"Really?"

"Yes."

"You're sure you want to go?"

"Yes."

"All right." He stooped gracefully and picked up my new handbag.

"Paul, I don't want you to think it's that we . . . you . . . I. . . ."

"That's OK," Paul said kindly. "Don't worry about it."

We buttoned our coats back up and went out to the elevator and down to the lobby and past the doorman's surprised face into Sunfield Street.

Paul walked me to Main. When we saw the Mechanicsville bus coming, he kissed me lightly, put the handbag in my arms, and asked, "Next Saturday?"

6 1

I had been terrified he wouldn't want to see me again. Gratefully I promised, "Next Saturday!" and climbed on the bus.

All the way home my body kept shouting silently Yes! Yes! Yes! and Beethoven boomed in my brain. But under the shouting and booming, Sister Teresa's voice spoke clearly: "Susan," it said, "Susan dear, this Paul is too much for you. He's too old for you and too rich and too worldly. And if you don't watch your step very, very carefully, you can get in too deep with him—too deep altogether."

December 29

DREAM

A bright garden. Pure, quiet air. Flowers like jewels hide in the grass. A blue waterfall sends a wavering stream through the garden.

Heavy seeds brush against my gown. They cling, then fall, scattering across rich earth as I walk toward a red-cushioned seat by the waterfall. Against the seat leans a heart-shaped shield marked ♀ .

I stand looking down at the shield, seeing it clearer and clearer— ♀ —whatever that means. A breeze lifts my hair and my white gown. The red-cushioned seat invites me; but still I stand looking at the shield.

Waking, I watch it fade away.

New Year's Eve

Aunt Millie offered to baby-sit, so Rianna and I could go
out tonight. "Sweet of her," Rianna said. "But where shall
we go?"

We discussed it. Movies are expensive and "jammed with
germs," as Rianna put it. We don't know a soul to visit.

"Maybe your Dad and Glory?"

"Ah . . . I don't know. . . ."

"That's OK. I was kidding."

We could slip into Ahmed's and sit and sip in the dark.
"Ugh!" said Rianna. "Tell you what, Sue. I'll read your
New Year cards."

So we thanked Aunt Millie anyhow, and here we sit in
Rianna's warm, cozy room, and she reads my cards.

I ask the question aloud firmly. "Will Elaine Richards
take Jason on for two years?"

Rianna shuffles the cards and fans them out before me on
the warm velvet, facedown.

Jason is good tonight. He leans against my feet chuckling
to Dada Bear, feeling Dada's ears and button eyes. He
crawls a little away and laughs up at me, waving Dada.
How *can* I want Elaine Richards, or anyone, to take him
away from me?

But I do! I've got to be free of Jason for two years, or else
live on welfare forever, entirely unable to learn, work, or
get ahead.

Slowly, left-handed, I draw my cards. I pray silently before each one. "Please, God, make this be the Happy Home card! Please make this one be the Children in a Garden card." Then my eye falls on Isis, in the middle of the table. I shouldn't pray here; it's sacrilege! I shouldn't be doing this at all, actually; the Devil is somewhere in it. Isn't that really why I use my left hand—"Let not your right hand know what your left hand does"? Holy Pat, it's all nonsense anyhow; it's a kids' game, with these colored cards! I could paint these pictures myself. If only they didn't make sense so often. . . .

I draw the last card, That Which Is to Come. Rianna turns the cards over, one by one, and lays them out like a cross; and each card, as she turns it, sears my mind.

The Bound Girl stands dejectedly beside a fence of swords. There's nothing she can do, there's nothing I can do.

Next is The Tower. Terrified men fall from a burning building; you can practically hear the screams. "It's the end," Rianna interprets happily, "the end of this phase of your life. After the end, you start fresh. Right?"

I don't know. Sometimes the end must simply be the end.

A sly fellow prances stealthily away from a sleeping camp. He carries off all their swords. "You have a plan," Rianna announces. I sure do! "It may backfire."

Now comes The Empress. She sits calmly in her bright garden, looking quietly out at the world. Her full lips are silent; her eyes are grave. Almost absent-mindedly she grasps her scepter, tipped with its mysterious ball.

As usual, Rianna is stumped. She shrugs, and wiggles expressive fingers. All she can say is, "She's what you want to be."

But what I want to be is *free*. And The Empress, ruling her garden, seems somehow bound to that red-cushioned

65

seat. She has been sitting there for centuries, you feel, and she'll be perfectly happy to sit there for centuries more with her scepter, her crown of stars, and her shield.

I look again. The device on the shield jogs a memory. "Rianna, what's that sign mean?"

"That's—hell, you know that. Everybody knows."

"Not me."

"It's . . . well, it's female. That's what it is, biological female. Male sign goes up like this"—she draws with her finger ♂ —"female goes down— ♀ —naturally." Bitterly!

"Oh." Yes, now I remember. ♂ , ♀ , Biology 1. But if that's all it is, why's it seem so important? Rianna shrugs again and passes on. "And here we have guess who? Your fairy godmother. You always pick The Queen of Swords, Sue."

That's because I've been abandoned. That upraised sword divides me from my past, my folks, from Paul and life itself. But it comes to me now, looking again upon that cold profile, that I am also abandoning. Here I am praying that Elaine Richards, that lovely lady who is Jason's astonished grandmother, will take him off my hands. I only mean for two years, of course, so I can get a start. But how can I be sure of getting him back then? Suppose Elaine got fond of him! Suppose she sued to keep him, because I was a delinquent mother or something. And haven't I been thinking about that suburban mansion of hers, and how safe and happy Jason would be there? Yes, I myself am The Queen of Swords.

But this is crazy! Holy Pat, I'm taking these dumb cards seriously!

Slowly, Rianna reaches for the last card, That Which Is to Come. This will finally answer my question, Will Elaine Richards take Jason? She turns it over. It is The World.

The embarrassingly bare lady skips in her Christmas

66

wreath. Rianna leans back, well satisfied. "You are going. The World means travel and assured success. That can only mean, Yes, Elaine will take Jason." For how else could I travel and succeed?

Jason hears his name. "Zuzu," he calls. "Awaaa!" He clutches my knee and pulls himself up.

I sit frozen, staring at The World. He sees I'm not paying attention to him; I'm doing something else. That maddens him. In an instant he turns from a smiling baby into a screeching monster: "Zuzu! *Awaaaa! Awaaaa!*" He arches his back, and his small fingers dig hard into my knee. He throws his head way back, so I'm looking right into his furious, howling mouth. "*Mamaaaaa!*"

"Jesus Christ!" says Rianna. She is disgusted.

Suddenly I'm mad. I want to scream and throw my head around, too. He never lets me alone! I can't do anything in the world apart from him! I'm so mad, I lift my hand to smash him.

Jason shuts up. Abruptly silent, he watches my hand. His brown eyes widen, his mouth hangs pinkly open.

My son is afraid—of me.

I seize him under the arms and haul him into my lap. I smooth his curls and cup his soft face in my hands and kiss it.

Rianna says, "You shouldn't have had him."

I look at her. It's true; I knew back then that Paul would leave me. I knew, but I didn't face it. I kept telling myself we'd work it out.

"You should have got rid of him," says Rianna.

I look at her through Jason's curls. Her eyes are hard; her thin hands move relentlessly, gathering the cards.

I almost agree with her. But then I don't. For this is one time Sister Teresa is right and Rianna is wrong. Back then, Jason was himself. Inside me, he was making these brown curls and eyes like Paul's. His pink mouth (still silent!) was

67

forming then, and the straight brows, like Mom's, and the chin dimple, like mine. And, of course, all the fantastic things we don't see—blood and brains and nerves.

Sister Teresa would have called him a creature of God. A guru Paul and I once heard lecture would have called him a child of the Universe. Paul called him an accident. Suppose Jason really was just that—a living accident in an accidental world in an accidental universe. Then, I guess, I could have got rid of him.

But then, of course, he would need all the more to be loved. An awful thing altogether, to be an accident!

Crooning I rock him, comforting us both.

And now I look at Rianna through Jason's soft dark curls, and I'm altogether glad I had him. *That* wasn't my mistake; *that* time, at least, I decided right. My blood and bones agree entirely.

But I say nothing of this to Rianna. Rianna has had an abortion.

Things Remembered

WINTER, TWO YEARS AGO

Every Saturday I spent with Paul. My folks thought I was at the movies with Maureen; and I *was* at the movies, only with Paul.

We always ended up at his place, and each time he touched me, my body cried Yes! and I said No. "That's all right," he would assure me. "Only when you want to, Suzanne."

But holy Pat, how I wanted to! Every night I dreamed of Paul. At first I tried to cover up those embarrassing dreams and forget them. Later I began to rerun them in my mind, and pretty soon I was daydreaming Paul. "How about me?" my body kept asking. "Don't I have rights?"

The day came when I told Paul, "I do want to! I really do. But it's dangerous."

"Dangerous?" Paul hid his smile.

"You know what I mean."

"Suzanne, love, have you never heard of the Pill?"

Of course I had heard of the Pill. Sister Teresa had a lot to say about the Pill. "But how would I get it?" I sure didn't see myself walking into a drugstore and asking for it! ("Can I help you, Miss?" "Yes, please, I'm looking for the Pill.")

"I've got it here." Paul actually drew it out of his pocket there and then and held it out to me. It was a plastic sheet of wee round white pills. I looked at them fearfully, with awe.

I whispered, "I can't take them. It's a sin."

"Why?" Paul drew near me. Electricity tingled between us.

"We're not married."

"So?"

I felt my way blindly through the theory. "So if there's a baby . . . he won't have a home." Or a father.

"But, love, if there's no baby, he doesn't need a home. See? That's what the Pill is for." Paul's arms closed around me like a trap. "So why is it a sin? Can you tell me why?"

"I . . . no."

"You know, Suzanne, I don't believe in God." Paul's hands burned on me. "But if I did, I'd sure ask him why he invented sex if it's a sin. It's his idea, you know." That certainly made sense.

Paul handed me the plastic sheet of pills, and I took it.

"Mom, what would you think if I had a boyfriend?"

Mom was washing dishes, I was drying. From the living room sounded the muffled roar of football. It was a dull Sunday afternoon.

Mom splashed suds. "I'd think you were too young."

"Mom, I'm sixteen! Maureen has a boyfriend."

"Thank God, I'm not responsible for Maureen. I'm only responsible for you. And I think sixteen is a bit young for that kind of thing." Mom added darkly, "Look at Mary Donovan!"

"Mary Donovan?" Come to think, Mary hadn't been to school lately. I hadn't worried. Mary was no great friend of mine.

"You're old enough to know, Susan." Mom lowered her voice and splashed louder. "Mary is having a baby."

Baby! An awful vision flashed like lightning through my mind. But then I remembered not to worry, I was safe. So long as I took the pills Paul had given me, nothing like that could happen to me. I had the pills hidden in my Sunday pumps in the back of my closet. And just in case Mom shook the pumps out, which wasn't too likely, I had de-labeled them. She would never guess what they were.

Mom was easy to fool because she trusted me. I would say I was seeing Maureen—who had been briefed—or studying at the library, and she would say, "Be home by ten, dear." Part of me wished I really was the sweet, trustable dear Mom thought I was. But most of me laughed proudly all the way to Paul's place. That furnished apartment with mounted photos and classical music on the hi-fi was a world entirely strange to my folks, a world where I was grown-up, independent, free. There I was sexy!

"How awful," I mumbled, stacking dishes. "So that's why Mary hasn't been to school!"

"School!" Mom snorted. "That's why she hasn't been home! They threw her out, the Donovans did."

I shivered, and the dishes rattled.

"Well, you really can't blame them," Mom went on. "It's a terrible disgrace; it's an insult to everything that family stands for. The *Donovans*, for Heaven's sake!"

That's right, I thought. Mr. Donovan was a lector at church. His sons—rough boys—were altar boys. Mrs. Donovan managed church suppers and fairs, and headed the sodality.

"They've stopped coming to church," Mom said, "they're so ashamed."

And this was the chance I was taking! If my folks ever found out about Paul, no pill could save me from their hurt, their astonishment, maybe their rejection!

But I was addicted to Paul. I loved him and his free life style, and the new me he was molding. If I didn't see him once a day, the sun would fall out of the sky.

Fooling my folks got steadily harder. "For all the study-ing you do at that library, you don't have much to show!"

71

Dad was disgusted at my report card. "Holy Pat, Suki, I might understand you flunking algebra, but *home ec?*"

"Do you feel all right?" Mom asked. "You haven't been painting lately. Your room's too neat, if you know what I mean."

"Home ec!" Dad fumed on. "Suki, are you sure you've been at the library all these nights?"

"Dan!" Mom shot him an indignant look.

We were having dinner, hamburg and peas and Mom's rolls, dripping butter. Dad faced me with this challenge. I know now it wasn't a real challenge at all. He didn't really think I had been lying; he was half kidding. But I was scared into a half-confession. "I'm sorry, Dad, I couldn't tell you. I was afraid you wouldn't understand."

Dad lowered his fork. "Wouldn't understand what?"

Mom turned to me, her eyes darkening.

"Well, I . . . I've been . . . seeing this boy."

Mom gasped.

"I was going to tell you, Mom, but you said I was too young—"

"*What Boy?*" Dad roared.

Most of the story came out then. They learned that Paul was no boy but a college man. And not a Catholic. And, no, I didn't think he wanted to meet them. All that was enough to shock and bewilder them entirely. I didn't mention that I spent my time in Paul's apartment. I figured that would give them heart attacks.

Dinner cooled while they lectured me. Dad growled about honesty and trustworthiness. Mom sobbed about purity and reputation. Both of them harped on the vicious character of college men, and especially of Paul. At that point I stopped listening. The bit about honor and purity had hit home, but the attack on Paul angered me. They didn't know Paul. How could they judge him? I wanted to say Judge not that ye be not judged, but I didn't. Their anger and grief twisted together in a terrific emotional tornado.

Dad finished, "And I'm sure I needn't say, You're not seeing the fellow again!"

"But, Dad—"

"No buts, my lady! No more libraries."

Mom shook her head at my protests. "Your father is entirely right, Susan. You've been playing with fire. You'd better go to confession."

And they didn't even know the bad part! The hamburg and peas and rolls went into the Disposal, and I ran upstairs to cry.

I never did go to confession. There's no point in confessing if you mean to go on sinning, and I did. I needed to prove to myself that I was not little Suki, a good youngster who could be protected and ordered around. I was sophisticated, worldly Suzanne. Because I didn't confess, I couldn't go to Communion. That hurt.

Paul had no patience with any of this. "Why don't you just move in with me?" he kept saying. "You can get a job, maybe finish high school nights. Be free and independent. I love you, Suzanne," he kept saying, "but I think you're a fool to let your parents run your life. You have to grow up someday, you know. They'll live with it. My parents do."

In the end I couldn't take the tension anymore. I decided Paul was right; it was high time I grew up. I was sick of hearing how young I was and how much I needed guidance! They didn't understand—my folks and Sister Teresa—that they were talking to an adult woman. I would have to show them.

Just after New Year's I packed a small bag. I brought it downstairs before dinner. The house smelled of pot roast and potatoes, but I did not hesitate.

Dad looked up from *Field and Stream* and asked suspiciously, "Going out?" Out in the kitchen, Mom heard. She came and stood in the hall by the Sacred Heart, wiping her hands on her apron. Under the apron her pantsuit was Christmas green.

I stood between them, ready to go. I said, "Mom, Dad, I'm sorry. I know you won't understand."

Dad lowered *Field and Stream.* I swallowed. "I have to go. I'm going to live with Paul—"

That was as far as I got. Dad leaped up. He hurled *Field and Stream* across the room—not at me. Veins stood out purple on his face and neck and wrists. In seconds he roared himself entirely hoarse. There was "Damned bitch" in it, and "Go on to Hell; we can't stop you," and "A life's work down the drain!" And finally, "Don't you come back here after this! Don't you darken this door again!"

I turned to Mom. She was bent over, weeping into her hands. I went to touch her, but she pulled away and drew back into the kitchen.

I left.

I walked out to Federal and caught the Springerton bus. At Paul's he kissed me and laughed, and we went out for lasagna. "Call them next week," he advised. "No sooner, or they'll think you're weakening. By next week they'll have come round."

But they didn't come round. When I called, Dad started yelling again. "I can get the law on you," he roared, "You know that? You're just sixteen; you're a kid!" Mom sobbed in the background. "You know what that goon of yours is doing is illegal? I can get the *law*, I tell you, Susan!" Not Suki anymore—Susan. "I don't run my family that way, I never have. Family business stays in the family. But I could get the *law*—and I damn well might, if you call and pester your mother. She's going out of her head!" The background noises cracked my heart. The receiver slamming down cracked my ear.

74

A week later I wrote a letter. Mom answered. In her gentle round hand she explained how they would always love me and pray for me, but they couldn't see me while I was living in sin. The letter was three lines long and signed "Your Mother" with a downward slope.

I got a job checking batteries. "You see!" Paul exclaimed. "Freedom is great."

In a way it was. It was great to know I could stand on my own two feet, with a nudge from Paul. I didn't have to be a good girl just to eat; I could make my own money. That was great. And I went on loving Paul and his—our—cozy place that sounded all day of Beethoven (I think).

But I never got over my folks. I never got used to not belonging at home. I couldn't stop thinking, "What would Mom think? What would Dad say?" About everything.

January 1

DREAM

I wander in a bright garden. The air is pure and quiet. A waterfall sings.

I walk slowly, careful not to crush the flowers that hide like jewels among the grasses. Heavy seeds brush against my gown. They cling, and fall.

Near the waterfall a shield leans against a red-cushioned seat. I see the symbol ♀ blazoned on the shield. Approaching the seat, I pause; I hesitate. A woman sits there.

Her flowing gown is white, red-embroidered. Loosely she holds up a scepter, tipped with a ball. As I stand watching, she turns toward me. Her full lips are silent; her eyes are grave; stars shine in her hair.

I am not exactly afraid. But I walk no nearer.

\

January 2, Afternoon

"Rent a car," Elaine had said. "I will reimburse you."

The car I've rented is an enormous Chevy. I've driven Paul's VW and Dad's pickup, but this is a whole new deal. You don't look down on the traffic, like in the pickup; you swim in traffic. All you can see is the rump of the car ahead, like in the VW. But you daren't pull past, because the Chevy's sides are so wide. Thank God, I don't have to park till I'm out in the country; I'd never squeeze this monster into a parking space!

Another thing—the Chevy is automatic. It's real easy, the garage man showed me how, and it's like a kid's toy but I keep reaching for the clutch that isn't there. And I'm terrified we'll stall, because—another thing—it's snowing. If we stop, I'm not at all sure we'll get moving again.

For now, we're doing fine, inching up Main behind another monstrous gas hog. Snow blows like fine dust; I can't see three cars ahead. I keep the wheels in the other monster's ruts. On both sides the snow is deepening fast. We pass several cars struggling out of parking spaces, spinning and whining. Holy Pat, a red light! God, make the car go when it turns green!

A few shoppers straggle across in front of us. Main is almost empty; some stores are closed. It doesn't look like the same busy street I saw before Christmas.

Jason is being good. The garage man liked Jason; he

77

actually brought out a little car seat for him and hung it beside me. Jason's sitting in it now, looking out at the shoppers. Dada Bear sits on the "steering wheel," looking at Jason. "Um," Jason says calmly when I glance his way. "Um, Dada."

The light turns green. I step very gently on the gas, the way Dad taught me, and sure enough she moves. We rumble cautiously past Federal and bear right on Hills.

Now the snow is softer, fluffier. It veers away from the windshield. We've lost our monster guide; we're making our own tracks. I navigate at twenty-five miles per hour. A funny happiness is creeping through me. It's been a while since I drove through the city. What this happiness is—it's a feeling of power! I'm in command here, and I'm doing nicely.

Now the houses are smaller and farther apart. Bare trees reach over roofs, and some yards have snow-fuzzed fences. In a minute we'll be out in the country. And then what? The driving's bad enough here; what'll it be in the country?

Jason is wiggling. I can't take my eyes off the road for a second, but I feel him squirming about. A soft thump tells me Dada has fallen off the "steering wheel."

"Quiet," I tell Jason. "We're almost there."

Jason murmurs, "Awa?"

"Just a few minutes." Maybe I can fool Jason, but I can't fool myself. It's a good half hour from here. It took Paul and me a half hour that summer day; and we weren't doing twenty-five miles per hour either.

I never take my eyes off the road. I see the snow flying at the windshield; I judge which rut to take and whether I can pass the oncoming truck. But I'm seeing a spring road, too. I'm remembering the trees leafy green, the fences bright with forsythia, kids playing with trucks and marbles in driveways.

78

A black cat bounded across the road, and I shivered. "Bad luck!" I said to Paul, half meaning it. "They won't like me."

I was scrunched in the passenger seat feeling sicker and sicker as the sidestreets turned into woods, and fields with horses.

Why was I so nervous about meeting Paul's folks? So what if they didn't like me! We weren't getting married, after all.

Only I thought we were. I still lived on the edge of my folks' world, the world I grew up in. That was a pretty simple, straightforward world. If a son brought a girl home, his folks thought he meant to marry her. They looked her over with that in mind.

So I had worn my best blue skirt with a white blouse and cardigan. That was the outfit Paul thought his mother would like. I had brushed my hair to its finest healthy-mouse sheen, and lipsticked my mouth modestly pink, and generally put on my best Renoir look. And I was twisting my hands together and sweating. I felt as if I were about to visit a foreign country which I had seen on TV and read about but where I didn't know the language.

Paul laughed. He took one tennis-strong hand off the wheel and covered my hands till they stopped twisting. "Don't worry!" he advised me coolly. "What do you care if they like you or not? Just be your sweet self."

That should have warned me! Those were definitely not the words of a son bringing home his bride-to-be.

"Anyhow, they'll like you. Depend upon it, Suzanne. Any friend of mine is a friend of theirs." Friend, huh? That again should have warned me!

Paul turned off the road. Aspen Lake gleamed behind huge, shadowy trees. A narrow road curved along the shore, with mansions set well back and far apart. You could shoot it out in one of those mansions, and no neighbor would hear you. I said "Paul, I'm sick. I'm going to—"

"Not here you aren't! What would the neighbors think?"

The Richards lived in a yellow palace that Paul called a garrison. The driveway swept grandly in toward the front door and out again to the road. Three tall evergreens stood in the curve like sentinels. At one end of the house was a glass porch where we sat with drinks and tried to talk.

I liked Mr. Richards right away. He was an older Paul—just as handsome but milder. I thought he must be a good boss to have; I wouldn't have minded working in his office. I couldn't imagine him either snarling at a secretary or chasing her around the desk. He would be altogether polite. "I'm sorry we have to let you go," he would say, not "You're fired."

Elaine Richards was cool and gentle, comfortable to talk with. She went out of her way to make me feel at ease, but she couldn't possibly approve of me. I could see that myself. Everywhere I stepped on her beige carpets I seemed to leave dusty footprints!

She must have known we were living together, but she never mentioned it.

Hey! Maybe she really didn't know! In which case I must have given her quite a shock, calling up about Jason.

There's the Aspen Lake sign now, half buried in snow. Asp La, it says. I know we bear right, but it's hard to see the road. I must have found it; we're still rolling. A faint rut leads us down to Aspen Lake, ice snowed over, with its bare trees and wide-spaced palaces.

We pass a brown palace and a brick one and a wild green one with balconies, and here stand three evergreens, twinkling Christmas lights. It's early in the day for lights; they must be a signal. I grit my teeth and drive in behind the evergreens where no driveway appears, and there, sure enough, is the yellow garrison.

I cut the engine. We're safe. If anything goes wrong here, Mr. Richards will just have to get us out. He won't want us in his hair overnight.

I pull out my comb from Millie's carryall and give my hair a lick. Then I climb out of the monster as gracefully as I can—which is good because Elaine is standing in the doorway, watching.

Elaine is tall and slender. Her gray hair curls short. She wears a white blouse and cardigan with a gray wool skirt. I wish I could have pressed my size-14 jeans! Graciously, she shows us into the living room.

The last time it was spring, and Paul and I passed through here on our way to the porch. This time I really get to see the room. It crosses the whole front of the house and opens on the porch, now glassed in, at the end. A Christmas tree stands out there, looking in. This is not just a Christmas tree; this is a royal Christmas tree! Its glass star brushes the high ceiling. Tinsel drips delicately, each strand carefully placed. Gold or red balls hang among the tinsel. Through the glass beyond, we see snow falling.

Jason and I perch on the edge of a brocaded antique chair by the fireplace, where a small fire flutters. Over the mantel hangs a large oil painting, gold and red swirls on dark brown. It doesn't say much. I suspect it was picked out to set off the room's colors.

The mantel is lined with Christmas cards and a large color photo of Paul. I stare at this, willing myself to feel nothing, not even hate. Paul looks at me over his shoulder. His dark eyes laugh; his mouth half smiles; he seems about to speak. But I don't let him. I look away at the grand piano—also bristling with Christmas cards—and back to Jason.

Jason is wide awake but silent on my lap. Thumb in

mouth, he gives Elaine solemn stare for stare. She sits on a hassock close to the fire. Leaning forward, she studies Jason.

I see the recognition in her eyes. Once she glances up quickly at Paul's picture as though to make sure, but she sees her little Paulie sitting on my lap, I know it as though she had told me so.

She stretches a slow hand out to Jason. He shrinks against me, and she withdraws it. "I wouldn't want to frighten him," she says. But I think it is she who is frightened.

"I brought out Pau—the old playpen," she says. "You needn't hold him." The playpen stands in the fire's warmth. It's lined with a cute-print quilt and a rubber duck.

I am touched. This is what I call thoughtful.

"Jason, look at the duckie! Duckie, see?" Hopefully I lower him into the playpen. It would be so lovely to sit like a lady and sip something without Jason grabbing for it.

Jason clutches the bars like a hysterical prisoner. He throws back his head and opens his mouth wide. Hastily I snatch him out and settle him back on my knee.

Elaine smiles understandingly. "In a little while, when he's used to the room, you can put him down. He's a lovely child, Suzanne. I will certainly have something to tell Mr. Richards when he calls!"

"Calls?" He's away?

"He went to Venice yesterday on business. He hopes to meet Paul in Florence."

So it's just the three of us. I had been counting on Mr. Richards as an ally; I remember him as kind and human. Elaine folds her arms as though she is cold, and looks at us sideways. Her eyes hold a gentle challenge; as if she would like to ask, "What do you want, Suzanne? You kept my grandson a secret for a year. Why do you come to me now?"

Politely I ask after Paul. I wish she would say, "He's had a bad bout with bubonic plague," but she assures me he is well. "He never writes, but he calls occasionally."

Both of us glance up at the photo. Paul glints back at us. He is the reason we are sitting here together, two uneasy women with nothing in common. He has bound us together with the living bond of Jason.

"Suzanne, would you like tea or coffee?"

"Oh, coffee, please."

Elaine fairly darts away to the kitchen. As the door swings, I glimpse shining steel and linoleum. Should I go after her, offer to carry things? I feel glued to the brocade, and I think Elaine is hiding from us, collecting herself. It must be rough to meet your grandson, already a year old, and have to be nice to his mother, who is a dumpy girl you never cared for, in crumpled jeans.

I inspect the room. This is where I want to leave Jason. I want him to learn to walk on this wall-to-wall beige carpet. He can hold on to polished chairs and a sofa with clawed feet, and beige lace drapes. (I see them torn down and trampled.) He can climb up on the stool and bang the piano. Who am I kidding!

But Elaine will know how to handle him. She's used to handling people; she enjoys it. Right now she's handling me, not altogether smoothly, but pretty well. I bet she could teach Jason to toddle around this museum without fingering an ashtray.

And think of the balanced meals that must come out of that stainless-steel kitchen in there! Think of the quiet bedrooms upstairs! I can easily imagine them. One has a view of Aspen Lake; another looks into the evergreens out front. One is Paul's old room, maybe still is, with his narrow bed and desk and prize photos. And I bet Elaine has his crib stored somewhere, too!

"Jason," I whisper, "I wouldn't mind a bit leaving you here."

Jason twists around to look up at me. His brown eyes are startled under Paul's curling lashes. Holy Pat, maybe he half understands! I am often surprised at how much he seems to understand. "But I'd miss you too much," I assure him. We rock gently on the edge of the chair. "Want to see the duckie?" Oh, to put him down!

"Awa."

"OK, OK. Just be quiet. Be good."

The door swings, and Elaine appears with a silver tray. She sets it down on the glass coffee table. I smell the rich steaming brew before I see it. And there's little party crackers and graham crackers for Jason, and a cheese log and sugar and cream and—a snifter!

"Would you like brandy in your coffee?"

I hesitate just a second. I do have to drive home through the snow, after all. But, with all those crackers. . . . "Yes, please!"

Elaine pours and passes. She hands me a little linen napkin; she spreads cheese on my cracker; she offers Jay a graham. He just looks at it. She offers me a cigarette, takes one herself, lights up, hunts for an ashtray. When she can fuss no more, she sinks down on the hassock and faces us. The time has come.

"How have you been, Suzanne?"

"Oh, fine. Thanks."

"Forgive me; we had better be frank. Does Paul send you money?"

"No. At first he did, but not now."

"Do you work?"

"No. I can't manage with Jason."

"I should think that might be difficult! How do you live?"

"We get welfare." Elaine winces. In this house, "welfare" is a dirty word.

"I will speak to Paul. He certainly must help you if—" She catches herself. She does not say, "If Jason is truly his child." She draws thoughtfully on her cigarette. "Have a cracker. Don't spare the cheese."

I don't spare it. I dive right in, spreading and munching. I'm starved! Jason reaches for a cracker—not a graham—my cracker. I give him one plain, and he sucks it, dribbling soft crumbs down his red sweater. I notice a few crumbs dropping carpetward, but I'm not going to pick them up while Elaine watches me through her smoke. Time to put her onstage instead of me.

"And how have *you* been, Mrs. Richards?"

"Very well indeed, Suzanne." She smiles. Her eyes crinkle the way Jason's do when he smiles. "I'm a working woman now, you know."

Working woman? "No, I didn't know that." This may well throw a monkey wrench!

"I manage the Bouquet Flowershop at the mall. I went to work fourteen months ago." Elaine twinkles at me.

I am so upset I stop eating. Here I thought I was dealing with a bored, middle-aged housewife, opening a door to an exciting new life for her, but I've been talking to a business woman.

"When Paul—ah—left home, the house seemed very empty. You know, Mr. Richards travels a great deal. Frankly, Suzanne, I lost heart for housework."

Elaine explains more. She married right after she graduated from Smith College and had Paul first thing. She stayed home with him all day and kept house. First it was an apartment, like Paul's and mine. Then it was a small house in a development, and then this Aspen Lake mansion. For twenty years Elaine sorted socks and polished silver and ironed shirts and sheets and made beds (I know she had a cleaning lady, but this isn't mentioned) and got Paul off to school with a good breakfast and Mr. Richards off to London with clean undies and planned two meals a day, three on holidays, and shopped for cufflinks and footballs and film (which she had to return because it wasn't quite right) and forgot entirely how to play the piano.

"I majored in piano at Smith, you know. I planned a concert career."

I am surprised! "Paul never mentioned anything like that."

Elaine shrugs gracefully and ashes her cigarette. "Paul may not know. While he was growing up I never touched the piano except to dust it."

Elaine felt guilty at the piano. She wanted to do right by her husband and son, she felt she ought to spend every living minute working for them. "The piano was just for me. And it took up my time . . . I could so easily have played all day and let the dishes sit in the sink!" So she gave it up, like a kid gives up candy for Lent. Only, this was a long, long Lent!

Then one day after Paul had grown up and gone, when the beautiful house stood empty and silent, Elaine sat down before the gleaming dustless keys and found she couldn't play! She'd forgotten how. "That whole side of me had died."

She smiles at my obvious shock. "Perhaps I sound bitter. I don't feel bitter; I know I did right. Paul was little; he needed me then, as Jason needs you now, more than anyone would ever need me again. No work on earth is more important than raising a child—certainly not playing the piano!

"But the day comes when the child grows up, and one is

86

free. One can wander about aimlessly, lunching with friends. I did that for a while. Or one can branch out, try for a new life."

I know I could never stop drawing, just because Jason didn't appreciate it! "You never went back to the piano?"

"Oh, yes, indeed, I have been relearning. I play Bach now as a hobby."

But for real life Elaine studied the want ads in the *Mirror* and came up with this flower shop. She took her courage in her two slender hands and went in and got the job. Within a year she was management. Now she leaps out of bed mornings, bolts down coffee and juice, and drives away to business. Mr. Richards has learned to boil his own eggs. The cleaning lady lets herself in with her own key.

Elaine leans forward to me. "I know how you feel now, Suzanne. You love your child, of course, but sometimes you wonder if he will *ever* grow up! Am I right?"

I nod. I have to smile, though I understand what Elaine is telling me. She has seen through my little trick; she knows I want out. And she's saying firmly that she isn't taking Jason on. There isn't room for him in her new life.

"But, you know, it happens so quickly! One day he's an adorable cuddle bug"—smiling at Jason—"and the next day he's a brusque young man with a moustache who doesn't want you in his life. And then you're free! You've done your job. You hope you've done a good job, but, good or bad, it's done. And you're free." Elaine settles back on her hassock almost purring with satisfaction. Mom would say she looked like the cat that swallowed the goldfish.

But I can't wait that long. The "next day" she's talking about takes twenty years. I can't drag around like this for twenty years; I'd end up in an institution!

I don't say any of this. There's no use. Elaine's face has been brightening steadily as she talks about her freedom. Her bright new face is as hard as Rianna's. She is determined not to sacrifice herself for us—and Holy Pat, why should she? I was the one who fell for her son and got pregnant. None of it was *her* idea.

We chat a while longer. We loosen up and talk almost like friends. Elaine shows me Paul's baby pictures—they might as well be pictures of Jason—and I do a pencil sketch of Jason for her to keep.

"Thank you," she says. "It's lovely. I'll show it to Mr. Richards, and he'll really know . . . what Jason's like."

Then she glances at her watch and snuffs her cigarette. "Now, Suzanne, let me give Jason a small Christmas present. Next year we'll know he's around, and we'll do better by him." You may not know where he is, though.

She goes over to an antique desk in the corner. While she writes a check, we polish off the crackers and cheese. Jason gets the last party cracker. I eat his grahams, and mop the goop off his sweater. I also pick some of the larger crumbs off the rug.

Elaine comes back with the check.

"Thanks, Mrs. Richards." With a stupendous effort I don't look at it. Is it enough to pay for the rent of the car? Elaine promised to pay for that, but she hasn't mentioned it. I just hope it's more than enough for a rubber duck!

"Give me your address, Suzanne. I don't want to lose track of you and Jason now we've all met."

"Well, actually, we're moving."

"Oh?"

"I'm going to art school in California."

"California! How envious you make me!" (Elaine asks no questions about Jason or about expenses, no "How will you manage?" She's entirely too smart for that.) "Sunshine, oranges, smog! But give me the school's address."

Even saying bye-bye sweetly to Jason, Elaine never touches him, not with the tip of a ringed finger. I think she is afraid of him, or of the claim his touch might make on her.

"Bye-bye," she calls again from the doorway. Jason watches her over my shoulder, squirming happily against me.

Thank God, the snow has stopped! As we climb into the Chevy and settle Jason and Dada in the car seat, a snowplow grinds past on the highway. Going back, the driving will be easier. As I put the key in the ignition, I hear a burst of triumphant piano music from the garrison. Paul would know if it was Bach.

Out of sight of Aspen Lake, I can't stand the suspense a moment longer. I see no car in the side mirror, and none coming. We are alone on the snowy road. I brake right there in the middle and pull out Elaine's check.

What is Elaine's idea of "a small Christmas present" for Jason?

It's fifty dollars.

Twenty dollars for the car rent, something for gas, twenty for a snow suit for Jason, six, seven dollars for . . . a rubber duck, I guess.

"Um," says Jason happily, swinging his feet. "Um, Zuzu." And he laughs.

I can't afford to cry, I'm driving. So I laugh with him.

January 2, Evening

"That rich bitch!" says Rianna. She is folding up the velvet cloth, wrapping the cards away in white silk. A client has just left.

Rianna unwinds her black turban and lets her hair fall free and rippling over the shoulders of her purple blouse. "You know what it is," she says, "it's the double standard. Her Paul's the innocent; you fooled him. Hey! I bet she thinks Jason isn't even Paul's kid."

"She knows he is. I saw her looking at him. They're like two peas in a pod." I look with pain at Paul's soft curls on Jason's head.

Jason has been playing with a saucepan and spoon in a fence of chairs. Now he pulls himself up, leaning on a chair seat, and looks back at me. Holy Pat, it's aba time!

Rianna's teakettle hisses on the stove. She moves toward it, her black skirt swinging as she walks. "I know what she wants you to do," she says. "She wants you to sacrifice your life, just like she did. She said how she cooked and kept house and all for twenty years? Hell, she got paid! She got her yellow castle in Lakeview, right?"

"Aspen Lake."

"She got three squares a day and a cleaning lady. What's she want? You won't get anything like that; you won't get anything. You'll do it on welfare. Hey, Sue, you believe that Venice-Florence story?"

Jason bangs his spoon on the chair and demands, "Aba!"

"Sure, I guess so." What does Rianna mean? "Wait, let me fix the aba."

"Well, I don't believe it. Would a contented husband go off to Italy at Christmastime, I ask you?"

I shrug. He might. I know nothing of the demands of business or of life at Aspen Lake. I lower the aba into the kettle.

"Not likely!" Rianna laughs. "You swallowed the sinker, Sue! That lady's been abandoned. She'd pick The Queen of Swords if she touched the pack!"

"Look, Rianna." I turn and face her. "I don't care all that much. It's not my business. I've got my own problems." God knows! "I just wish she had come up with a few more dollars—that would have been only fair."

Jason roars. I stomp over there, snatch him up, and rest him on my hip. He flings himself sideways, still roaring. Rianna watches us.

Her silent comment is embarrassing. I slink back to the stove and test the milk on my wrist the way Aunt Millie taught me. It's still cold, of course, but I'm desperate. I shove it at Jason anyhow. He tastes it eagerly, then knocks it aside, and yells louder. Back in the kettle it goes.

Rianna says, "If he's getting his aba, we may as well get tea."

I have heard of a Japanese tea ceremony. We had one once at Holy Name, in costume. Anyhow Rianna has her own tea ceremony. With slow, religious-type gestures, she crumbles herbs in a basket woven from a certain kind of wood. Then she pours the boiling water—not quite boiling, just beginning—on it and lets it steep for a particular while. Meanwhile she makes witchy gestures over it—you'd swear she was praying. Finally she pours the brew into porcelain cups. Plastic won't do for Rianna's sacred tea. This evening she pours it into one porcelain cup and into the mug I gave her. I like to see her using it.

I try the bottle on Jason again. This time he smiles, and drinks. Now we'll have peace—maybe ten minutes of it.

We sit at the round table, the tea steaming before us. Jason is quiet on my lap, his head on my breast, watching us while he drinks. His warm weight calms me; I relax enough to smell the tea—camomile and mint. Alone I'd gulp it down in a minute, but with Rianna that would be an insult. We sip and savor.

After a while I ask, "Rianna, what can I do?"

She nods toward the white-silk package of cards. "We'll ask."

"Can't *you* think of something I can do?"

"Hell, yes!" comes the surprising answer. "But you won't like it."

"Try me!"

"You've looked everywhere. You've tried everybody."

"Everybody that has any reason to take an interest."

"What about other people? What about the Family Service?"

"My Dad mentioned them."

"But you haven't tried them. Why not?"

"I'm not sure why. I really don't want to."

I'm shy of lugging my baby along to strangers, asking them to take him on. I'm ashamed—that's it. And I don't blame myself. After all, I haven't been able to ask anybody outright, even the grandparents. I've just hinted and accepted their hinted refusals.

"OK. You're sure you have no forgotten aunt?"

"I'm not going to ask Aunt Millie!"

"Calm down. What about a long-lost sister?"

"My only sister is you."

Rianna shoots me a long look over her mug. Her eyes are warm. For a second they deepen, and I glimpse another dimension behind them. Rianna, who loves no one and makes no friends, loves me. I am her sister, and she is mine. "And I'm no good for this," she says.

"Oh, I didn't mean I'd ever ask *you*—"

"Sue, before you start even thinking about it, let me tell you. You couldn't ask anybody worse than me. I'll tell you why."

"But I'm not—"

"Just let me tell you. Then you'll know my idea for you, too."

Rianna sets her mug down and glances at Jason as if she's worried he might hear. He is drowsing, his head heavy on my breast. Softly, looking at Jason, she tells me.

I used to be shocked about Rianna's abortion. Then I got used to the idea and accepted it. It was just part of Rianna, my friend. Now I am shocked again, shocked and shaken. I am glad that Rianna is looking at Jason and doesn't see my eyes. I wouldn't want her to see my amazement, disbelief, horror.

What Rianna tells me is that she had another child, too—an older one. "A little older than Jason. I had to let him go, Sue, and I didn't have anybody, not a soul in the world."

I know that's true. Rianna grew up in foster homes. She has never gone back to visit any of them. "And where I lived then, they didn't have Family Service, or I didn't know about it. Well, I tried Carl's folks." She laughs bitterly. "They didn't want him; they said he wasn't Carl's kid!"

Jason squirms and drops his bottle. I have been hanging on to him, squeezing him. "Awa!" he squawks. I pick up the bottle, give it back, relax my hold a bit. "So what did you? . . ."

But Rianna waits till Jason's eyes slide shut.

93

"Well," she says then, "he was older, you know. He could walk. You know what a kid does when he can walk? He walks away." Again she laughs that pained, brief laugh. "So I let him."

I swallow. A picture is forming in my mind, but I can't believe it. "How, exactly? . . ."

"In the supermarket. I let him down off the cart and stood him on his feet, and he walked off like a windup toy!" Rianna falls silent. She looks not at me but into her mug, which is empty.

"And then?"

"I walked away, too."

Sweat is sliming my shirt. "You don't mean—"

"I do mean. I walked out the door. I meant to just take off, but . . . I couldn't do that. I hung around to make sure."

Rianna is ashamed, not that she walked off, but that she didn't walk all the way off at once. She hung around to make sure. That cold, quiet ferocity of hers is real, no act. She's a whole real person, not like me. Sometimes I talk bold so I'll feel bold. Not Rianna. Rianna is truly as hard as she seems.

I stare at her, horrified and respectful. An enormous respect for her mushrooms in my heart, like the feeling I used to have for Brendan Kelley. My Dad had this friend, Brendan Kelley, who was in the Big War—they were in it together. Brendan killed four Germans with one grenade, and he used to boast about it. But I couldn't help wondering about the Germans. Suppose each German had a wife and a kid, and two parents, and maybe a brother and sister—that's six people each. Six times four is twenty-four; plus the four Germans themselves, that's twenty-eight people Brendan Kelley did for. I wondered if he ever thought about them. He seemed very much a whole man, entirely proud of his big real-life adventure. I respected him

94

for walking around so proudly with twenty-eight people on his conscience.

That's how I feel now about Rianna. I don't know if I could do what she has done. I glance down at Jason. His weight isn't reassuring enough; I need to see him! He is sound asleep; the empty aba lies across his elephant-patch knees. I place it very gently on the table.

Rianna sighs. "Hell, it's a civilized world. A kid can't toddle around a supermarket by himself; he gets picked up."

"Did your. . . ."

"Believe me, there was a hoo-ha in that supermarket! They had a loudspeaker, I heard it out in the street. That's when I left."

"Then you never knew. . . ."

"I knew. They had him in the papers, front page, like a lost pooch. *Is this pooch yours?* They took him to City Hall."

"And then?"

"That's as far as I followed the case. It's a civilized world, Sue, no matter what it looks like. They don't let a pooch starve if they can catch him, nor a kid, either."

I wish I had a pencil; I'd draw Rianna right now. That arrogant eye, the haughty lift of the lean chin—they're downright beautiful because they're real. The way a desert is real, or the barren moon. No, come to think, I wouldn't *draw* Rianna; I'd scratch her portrait—white lines in black ink—like a woodcut, cold and stern. So this is the secret of Rianna's freedom. Rejection is the price of freedom.

Rianna stands up. She takes our cups to the sink and comes back with the velvet cloth. Half laughing into my shocked face, she asks, "Do you still want me to read your cards?"

Holy Pat, yes! If Rianna is as real as I now know she is, then her cards are real, too. Isis, or something, really does speak through her cards. "More than before."

She nods. She winds the black turban over her hair, spreads the cloth, takes up the cards. She sits down with me and smooths her wide-flowing skirt.

Five minutes later, the cards stand revealed: The Tower, the screaming, falling men; The World, success and travel; and the last, most important card, That Which Is to Come. Together, we stare at it. Rianna is taken aback. "The Empress," she breathes. "Ah, *m-hm*."

"What does she mean?" This time I need a clear answer.

"Hard to say. . . ."

Rianna indeed seems to find it very hard to say. Her eyes flit from one card to another; she touches them all, one by one, with light fingertips. The Empress watches us calmly. She sits in her bright garden, the ♀ shield beside her. Her robe flows like the waterfall; stars glow in her hair. Her lips appear ready to open, to tell us the meaning we cannot guess. Meaning surrounds her like a thinning mist. It's as though the card was an unfocused slide; sharpen the focus only a little, and the picture becomes clear. Only we can't find the mechanism. . . .

Rianna lays her whole hand, palm down, across the card.

"What are you doing?"

"Sometimes I can feel a meaning. . . ." She gives up. "Not this time. Well, look, The Empress can mean action."

"Action?" A vague meaning!

"Maybe an action of the kind we were talking about. Or maybe she might mean . . . something hidden. Yes, that's it!" Rianna brightens. "Hidden! Isis hasn't decided yet, Susan. Your future is still hidden."

Well, Holy Pat, the future is always hidden! That's what tarot cards are for—to reveal what is hidden, to "make the high way low and the rough way smooth." Rianna is cheating. She knows what The Empress is saying; she just doesn't want to tell me.

I look up at her, ready to argue, and I notice a strange

96

thing, a thing that stops me cold. Rianna is holding the Empress card upright in her fingers, looking stiffly down at it. Her profile is cold and proud. Her pose reminds me strongly of another tarot card, an all too familiar card!

Rianna is herself the living image of The Queen of Swords.

Things Remembered

SPRING, ALMOST TWO YEARS AGO

"Suzanne," Paul said, "You look a fright."

Startled, I glanced down at myself. It was Sunday morning and I was lounging on the couch, idly sketching the fall of light through the window with its complications of shadow and half shadow. I had on my workclothes—jeans and a boy's shirt—because they were comfortable. That must be what Paul meant. Nothing else showed. It was much too early to show in any way; I wasn't even sure about it yet myself. "You don't like this outfit? OK, I'll change." Paul's *thing* about neatness was hard to live with. I was not naturally neat, and even after having lived with him for three months, I still kept forgetting and being careless till he reminded me.

"It's not just the clothes," he said now. "It's you. Have you stepped on a scale lately?"

Oh, that. I was getting decidedly heavy. I feared it might be part of the . . . secret. Maybe eight, nine times a day I would worry about the secret, and worrying always made me hungry, ravenously hungry. I mumbled, "I can always go on a diet."

"Of course you can, love. But I wonder if you will. See, I think you're trying to punish me."

"*What?*" What could he mean by that? Could he possibly have guessed the secret?

"Unconsciously, of course. You think you can punish me

by being less attractive."

I breathed again. He was just lecturing as he did so often—I was beginning to wonder if Paul really knew all that much about all the things he lectured on. "Why don't you quit photography, Paul? Take up psych?"

"Suzanne, I'm serious." Paul came over and sat on the couch beside me. He took the sketch pad out of my hands so he could hold them. "You are really going downhill. You are in a state of spectacular decline."

"Hey, thanks!" Decline was not the word for it, if Paul had only known! It was actually a very quiet, unspectacular *beginning.*

"You're fattening yourself up like a squirrel for winter. You wear those ghastly duds around the place—you'd wear them out to dinner if I'd let you! And you know yourself I'm always picking up after you." He nodded around at my scattered pencils, sketches, and saucers of crumbs.

Paul was right. I never was great for housework, and since the secret, I was feeling queasy. It was all I could do to check batteries for eight hours, without coming home to neaten up the apartment.

"You're letting yourself go in all directions at once," Paul said. "And I think, I *think,* you're doing it to get back at me."

I stared into his warm brown eyes. "For what do I want to get back at you?"

"For one, because I made you grow up."

"I love you for that!" And I did; I still really did.

"With half your mind. With the other half, I think you hate me."

"Unconsciously?"

"Of course."

"Well, I don't know about all that stuff. See, I dropped out of school—"

"So you do have a grudge against me!"

99

"But I know I love you, Paul. If you want, I'll change into a skirt."

"No rush." Paul squeezed my hands and let go. "Finish your sketch. But don't start the next one till you look human, OK?"

So that day was all right. Paul did not guess then. I wore my linen-look skirt, and we went out to a salad bar.

But over the next month I kept getting heavier. Paul did most of our cooking when we ate at home. He was an amateur chef. He fixed thinning meals anyhow on principle—broiled chicken, drained tuna, sprouts, and mushrooms, always with salad, salad, salad—and now he took special care to thin me down. But I got no thinner.

"You think you're getting back at me," he insisted.

"I do *not!*"

"But you're just hurting yourself. Can't you see that?"

"I am not! I'm hungry, Paul, *hungry!*" I wanted to wail, "I'm pregnant, Paul, *pregnant!*" By then I was sure.

"Have a diet soda."

"Ugh!"

Maybe—it's just possible—Paul was righter than he knew, and I really was trying to punish . . . someone. I've never been sure just why I stopped taking those little white pills. I certainly did hate them. I thought of cancer when I took them, and blood clots, and sin. And I didn't see why I should be the one to take all the precautions. Why couldn't Paul do something himself? He said it was easier this way. Well, it was easier for me to forget those awful pills! I forgot them a couple of times, and then another couple of times, and then it happened.

At first I was worried sick and scared to death. Then when I was sure, I began to wonder at this amazing thing that was happening to me, little Suki. A spark of life had struck inside me and burned there, day and night, without my knowing or doing a thing about it. I remembered Biology 1 and pictured the life inside looking like a fish, or maybe a tadpole, turning more human every day. I didn't know if it had eyes yet, or fingers, and I didn't need to know. God took care of all that. All I had to do was shelter it.

But I couldn't shelter it entirely alone. One night I whispered in Paul's ear as he fell asleep, "Paul. I'm going to—I mean—I'm pregnant." He didn't answer me. He didn't turn his head or twitch a muscle. He just lay there. "Paul? Did you hear me?"

Very quietly, "I'm not deaf."

"What do you . . . how do you like it?"

Very quietly, "What the hell do you mean, how do I like it?"

"What do you, ah, think about it?"

"I think I'll have to ask my parents for a raise." At last Paul moved. I thought he was going to take me in his arms, but he turned his back on me. A minute later—much too soon to be convincing—he snored.

Ask his parents for a raise? That was a funny answer. I lay thinking about it, wondering exactly what he meant.

I found out next day. I had barely gotten in from work and dropped my jacket on the sofa when Paul waltzed in, whistling.

"It's OK," he said. "I got the money." He kissed me and turned to pick up my jacket. "*Don't* leave stuff lying around, Suzanne. I didn't tell the parents why I wanted it, of course; they thought I needed a raise anyhow. So then I went to see Amy, and she gave me the address."

Confused, I floundered. "What address?"

"The clinic. Amy's a whizz—she even called and got you an appointment Saturday."

"Appointment? For what?"

"For an abortion. What do you think? You weren't kidding last night, were you?"

Paul opened the closet door and fished out a hanger. He hung my jacket up neatly, and turned to look at me. "Were you?"

I sank down on the sofa. I was worn out and queasy, and shocked into silence. It was amazing that Paul, who was so fussy about little things like hanging up clothes, should be so grandly careless about a big thing like this.

To please Paul, I had ripped a lot of stitches out of my life. God and my folks had gone to the dump. Paul had torn all the pages out of my book of rules and tossed them to the winds. But the rule we were now suddenly talking about was not written in any book; it was written in my body. I breathed deep and found I had a voice. It said, "I could never, never, never, do that!"

Paul sighed. "Don't go religious on me, for God's sake; I'm sick of it!"

"Holy Pat! What's religious about having a baby?"

"Suzanne, you don't need to have it. I've got the money."

"Money can't help." For once I was angry! For once I looked cross-eyed at Paul. A spark of life was burning, and he wanted to snuff it out, just like that. The only objection he could see was money. If you had the money you could do anything—that was Paul's idea. "Paul," I said slowly, "I don't think you understand. We are going to have a baby."

"*You* are going to have a baby—if you're that stubborn." Paul slipped off his own jacket and hung it up neatly. "Just remember it was your decision, and don't come blaming me."

Well, now, I had heard of male chauvinism, but this! "Now look, Paul, you're in this pretty deep!"

"The hell I am!" Paul swung around to face me. "Let's just look at the facts." He counted them on his fingers.

102

"One, I get you pills. Two, you forget to take them. Three, you get pregnant. Four, I offer you an abortion. Five, you refuse. The decision is yours, Suzanne; it's on you. *I have nothing to do with it!*"

Well, I must say, it was not the reaction I had hoped for. In Maureen's confession stories, when the girl said, "I'm pregnant," the man said, "Let's get married." Something more or less on that order was what I'd had in mind.

I was disappointed, shocked, and dreadfully hurt. I said silently to the spark of life, "Never mind, I'll take care of you." And my blood and bones and nerves agreed.

Only I began to see that it might be difficult.

Things Remembered

DECEMBER BEFORE LAST

The pains began in the evening, over at Amy and Aaron's. We were sitting around on floor cushions, drinking wine, and listening to classical. Nobody noticed I wasn't talking. I never talked much there. I felt like a dumb school kid with those people. They were Paul's age, his friends.

I put my wine glass down on the floor and gave the weird feelings in my spine all my attention. If I went glassy-eyed, no one noticed. I knew this was it. Dr. Armstrong had told me what to expect. I could feel a door inside me creaking slowly open to let the baby out. Fear froze me.

I glanced at Paul. Head bent, he was conducting the music with one hand. I dreaded trying to tear him away. He would be bored, impatient, annoyed.

Paul was already bored with the whole business. He hadn't even wanted me to go to Maternity! "It's a perfectly natural thing," he kept saying. "You probably won't even need a doctor." He seemed to think I would have the baby some afternoon, and then in the evening we'd go out and see a show.

Looking back now it's hard to believe how dumb we both were—not just Paul, but me, too. I knew something big was going to happen to my body; I was scared to death. But I just never thought my *whole life* would change! I bought six wee nightgowns for "it," and a blanket, and a plastic laundry basket for "it" to sleep in, and beyond that I didn't think.

Paul didn't think even that far. He just never thought about this business at all.

Amy took my side. I remember that now, when I hate her too much. "Something might go wrong," she said. "You don't want the responsibility, Paul."

Paul finally saw it my way, and I went to Maternity and Dr. Armstrong. By that time I was altogether enormous. Dr. Armstrong figured the baby was due in two more weeks, but she did not scold me for coming in late. Gently she explained what would happen and what I should do. And she promised to be there with me.

Her promise cheered me as I sat there in the noise— Beethoven, Brahms, whoever. I longed for Dr. Armstrong! I longed for Mom, too. For nine months I had been wanting to call Mom up and tell her what was happening to me. But I remembered Dad's rage and Mom's tears, and her final letter. And all that had happened before any baby was thought of! Now, it would have to be worse. That's what I thought.

Amy muttered to Paul under the music. Paul glanced over at me. "You OK, Suzanne?"

"Yes, I—no. No! Please, Paul, let's go!"

Paul was a pretty fast driver, but I never saw him drive that fast! Maybe he had taken it lightly before, but when he saw me doubled over, gritting my teeth, he really stepped on that gas. We fairly tore through the dark streets to Maternity.

Then I was alone with my pain in a high white room that smelled sterile. The pain grew and grew, and I prayed. Panting, I called on Mother Mary, and Mom, and Dr. Armstrong. Dr. Armstrong came.

She was gray-haired and soft-spoken. Her hands on me

were warm and firm. She quieted me, so I could understand what she was saying. Then she gave directions, and I followed them. The huge white clock said five hours had passed when it seemed like five minutes. Later the clock said five minutes when it seemed like five hours. Jason was born when the clock said five forty-five.

Dr. Armstrong lifted him in her hands to show me. She called him a "wee boy," but he looked enormous to have been inside me! He weighed six pounds something. I laughed with relief. Jason's round dark face screwed up for his first cry. He cried; I laughed; Dr. Armstrong and the nurse bustled softly about.

Later, when I got to hold Jason, I felt how really wee he was. His silky skin was dark and blotched, creased and crumpled. He had only a few wisps of dark hair. Only his wide sleepy eyes seemed really human.

Dr. Armstrong showed me how to nurse him. My breast touched his soft lips, and they opened. They opened, accepted, sucked. His roving eyes met mine. "He doesn't really see you," Dr. Armstrong told me. But he did see me; he did! I saw his eyes seeing me, and I bent to him, and love welled up in me like milk.

Right then I knew that no one and nothing in the world mattered more to me than Jason. I longed to show him my love, show him he needn't worry about that weird world out there because I would look after him. I would have liked for a lion to walk in right then and sniff at him, so I could have torn the lion in shreds with my two hands. But only Paul walked in.

He looked at me curiously, with relief. He didn't look at Jason at all until I pointed him out. "Paul, meet Jason."

Paul gave the mite a hasty glance; then he said, "Jason? Where'd you get that name?"

"From my grandfather." Jason Delaney.

Paul smiled and shrugged. He had not been interested

106

enough to discuss Jason's name before his birth. He never really fell for him after. The idea of being a father had bored Paul; the fact angered him.

To Paul, being a father came to mean not going out, not having Beethoven on loud, not making love, not seeing shows, not even sleeping through the night. He would grumble, "How can anything that small make so much noise!" He would growl, "If I had had any notion of how it would be!" He would swear, "If marriage is anything like this, I'm never getting married!"

Anxiously I wondered if he meant it. When I got too pregnant, I had quit work, and now Jason and I were living on Paul's money. Altogether apart from wanting Paul himself around, we really counted on that money! What would we do if Paul got too tired of fatherhood? What would he do—just walk out?

Paul stood it for three months.

January 4, Late Morning

How do you ask someone, Please take over my baby for me?

I haven't been able to ask Jason's grandparents that. How can I ask strangers? Would a bold approach work? "Look, I'm too young for this. I can't be saddled with a kid; I *am* a kid!" Or should I stare at the floor and whisper, "Please help me, I can't cope." How about a cool "I'm a taxpayer, after all"? (Only, I'm not.)

I don't know how to say it but now there's just a day and a half left, and here we are in the dragon's cave, the Family Service reception room. It's smaller than I expected. Steep, narrow stairs lead to this little room with soft chairs, toys on the floor, and a middle-aged woman receptionist. She sits at a large desk, sorting papers and answering the phone.

I came in here slowly, sort of shaky, with Jason like an awkward package on my hip. She smiled at us, took down both our names, and asked us to wait to see the "intake worker."

The room is warm. I peel off Jason's jacket and my coat. Now Jason notices the toys. I have brought Dada in my carryall just in case, but Jason is perfectly happy talking to a panda on the floor. I sit down, and they lean against my leg.

This receptionist must answer the phone twice a minute. I guess there are a lot of people in trouble, people who can't cope; it isn't only me. This woman takes serious problems for granted. Calmly she files appointments, calls the police, gives first-aid advice. "For now, let him sleep it off. Bring him in Thursday." Somebody's having hysterics on the other end of the line. "We can send in a case worker. Mrs. Pattie will know. . . . All right. Let us know. Bye, now."

It's like in the hospital. Nobody gets excited about pain; it's taken for granted. You can writhe like a snake and scream like crazy, and that's all in the day's work. They just take care of you, and go on to the next case. And you say to yourself "Hey, this pain must be normal. They've seen it before." And you relax.

I'm beginning to relax here. The phone rings constantly, and this nice woman answers mildly, takes care of it, and goes on to the next case. To her, Jason and I are a case. She sees cases like us every day.

I'm almost relaxed when a door I hadn't noticed opens and out comes a pretty blonde. She's a bit older than Rianna, and she's wearing a tweed skirt suit and high heels. She stops at the desk and murmurs with the receptionist, and then she comes over to us.

"Hello," she says gently, "I'm Mary Alden, I'm the intake worker for Mrs. Pattie. Let's go in the office."

The office is small, lined with books. There is no phone on the desk, only a pad and pencil. Jason sits on my lap now, watching Mary Alden and sucking his thumb. I face her across the desk. I'm less worried, now. I bet I could say, "I want to put this baby up for adoption," and she'd just nod and write it down.

"Ms. O'Hara. May I call you Susan?"

"Oh, yes." A good beginning.

"Call me Mary."

"OK."

"Now, Susan, what kind of help do you feel you need?"

Beautiful altogether! We come in cold off the street, and

109

this gentle stranger asks us what help we need, just like that! Suppose I said, "I'd like a thousand dollars," or "I'd like a Bermuda vacation, please"?

I hear myself say in the quiet, steady voice they use around here, "I need a home for Jason for two years."

"A temporary foster home?"

"Yes. That's it."

"I see. Why do you need this?"

"Because I have to go to California. I've got a scholarship." I tell that story. Mary Alden scribbles on her pad. Mothers must be coming in and ordering foster homes every day; it's business as usual.

"Well," she says, "we have a number of foster homes. We may have a vacancy in two or three weeks. If you would—What is it, Susan?"

"Two or three weeks?"

"Perhaps ten days."

"I have to leave day after tomorrow!"

Surprise flickers for just a second in Mary's eyes. "Oh. I didn't realize this was an emergency."

"Well, yes. It really is."

"I see. Excuse me, Susan. I'll be back in a moment."

Mary Alden goes out another door I hadn't noticed. A faint sound of typing comes through that door, and a phone rings.

"Zuzu," Jason murmurs. "Awa."

"I'm here, Jason." He cuddles against me.

It's true, just as Rianna said, this is a civilized world. I could walk out of here now, and when Mary Alden came back and found Jason by himself, she'd just . . . handle the matter. I know she would. Jason would be fine. I bet it happens all the time.

Mary Alden comes back, shaking her head. "There's simply nothing open right now, Susan. But in two weeks certainly—maybe sooner. Meanwhile let's get the facts all down—the vital statistics."

I answer her questions, and she takes it all down: "Grandmother missing . . . Grandfather 60½ Oak . . . Grandmother? Aspen Lake . . . Mother seeks education . . . Friend Rianna, One one four State . . . No disability. Phone number?"

"We don't have one."

"All right, Susan. You can call us next week. Mrs. Pattie will be back then. I realize it's hard to scramble your plans, but. . . ."

What Mary Alden doesn't know is, I'm not scrambling any plans. I am leaving the sixth. But if I have to, I can leave Mary a surprise. She can handle it.

I walk out as satisfied as a burglar who finds a rich house unlocked. Here is a wealth of kind, civilized concern I never knew existed! I won't have to put my Jason down in a supermarket and stride away, like brave Rianna, and never know who picks him up. When worse comes to worst, this door will be open.

Rianna wouldn't hesitate a minute. But I am not brave. The thought of leaving Jason, even with Mary Alden, sets me shivering.

Things Remembered

LAST JANUARY

"I'm sick of this!" Paul rasped angrily.

"What now?"

"I'm sick of the mess you make of this place!"

I looked around. The apartment was no more a mess than it had to be. Jason had to sleep somewhere; we had him neatly tucked in a laundry basket in the far dark corner. His few worldly goods—nightgowns, blankets, and disposables—had to be stored somewhere. They only took up the sock drawer of the bureau. Paul's socks were piled on the floor behind the armchair.

"Suzanne, face it! You're an amateur. You've got a nerve, spreading your damned art stuff to hell and back!"

Our walls were pretty well covered with my pictures. But I had asked Paul long before if he minded sharing wall space with me, and he had said, "Of course not. You live here, too."

Now he said, "I'm the professional around here, but you leave oil tubes in the armchair so I'll sit on them and newsprint pads on the coffee table, and—"

"OK, OK. There's things I'm sick of, too!"

Paul sneered, "What's your gripe?"

"I'm altogether sick of you bringing in your loudmouthed friends in the small hours waking Jason—"

"I'm sick of Jason, too! Why did you go and have an

accident like that? Amy says you did it on purpose, so I'd marry you."

"And I'm altogether entirely sick of Amy!" I hurled my voice at him. "I never want to hear another word of what Amy says!"

"Well, that's too bad, because I'm going over to Amy and Aaron's right now." Paul relented an inch. "Why don't you come, too? Be friendly for a change."

"How can I? Jason—"

"They don't mind if you feed him there."

"But I do!" Nursing my baby in public was too embarrassing. I felt naked. Maybe if I had *liked* Amy and Aaron, it might have been different. "Besides, it's not good for him to be hauled around. He should sleep in his own bed."

"Yeah, yeah." Paul darted about picking up stuff to take with him: proofs, Aaron's tapes, Amy's sweater. "It's always his feeding time or his sleeping time; we never get to go anywhere. OK, Suzanne, you stick in this hole if you want. I'll be damned if I'll stick in it with you!" Paul left, and slammed the door.

Jason started awake in his basket, and whimpered. I lifted him out and paced the messy room with him warm and wet in my arms. His chin bobbed on my shoulder, his soft cheek brushed my neck. I cried.

I hated being left, especially at night. Out on Sunfield, cars honked, girls my age met friends and went to the movies, or dancing, or to play basketball. Three streets away, Paul laughed and chatted with Amy and Aaron. Maybe they were going off to a movie. And I wandered the apartment wall to wall with this helpless bundle of love in my arms.

I sank down on the couch and nursed Jason. His soft lips caught my breast eagerly; he waved his little hands with joy. My teary gaze wandered around the apartment. Paul was right; it was a mess! I just never had the energy to work at it. Sketches and disposables lay all around with socks and tubes of oil paint. The dishes were dirty, the bed unmade. Worst of all, my drawings took up every inch of wall space. Without meaning to, I had pushed Paul's photos right off the walls.

Maybe, I thought, if Paul came home to a neat, clean apartment he might feel friendlier. Instant, purposeful energy came alive in me. I laid satisfied Jason down in his basket and tore into the work.

I made the bed. I washed dishes and dried and stacked them. I dusted the coffee table, scrubbed stove and sink, smoothed the chair throws, and stuffed my art materials into the kitchen cabinet. This left the pots and pans out in the cold. I let them sit in the sink, low profile, while I thought where to put them. While I worked, LUV sang on the radio, and I hummed the tunes. I hummed "Never Leave Me" as I carefully took my drawings off the walls, and "You Are My Springtime" as I hung Paul's most live-withable photos. (No public buildings, no nude Amy. I chose his portraits of Jason and me, clothed, and an Aspen Lake birch tree.)

I stood back then and looked happily at my work; and I saw that it was good. Neat and almost clean, the apartment glowed homey in the soft lamplight. I pushed the armchair back to the wall over Paul's socks, and neatened the pile of disposables next to Jason. There! I couldn't wait to see Paul's face when he came home!

At eleven o'clock, tired and proud, I took a shower and made myself a small salad. Paul would approve of that. Then I stretched out on the sofa to wait. "I'll Love You Forever," LUV sang softly.

I dozed and dreamed Paul came home looking around amazed. And I sensed someone else in the room. "Who's there?" I called out.

"Just me. Didn't want to bother you." I came awake, and there was Paul in the flesh, moving about quickly, taking things out of drawers and corners.

I sat up and saw that he was piling his shirts in the armchair. "Paul! What are you doing?"

"Packing."

"Oh, no! Oh, you can't!" What I most feared in my deepest heart was happening. But surely I could find words or actions to fend it off. "You wouldn't!"

Paul folded his tennis sweater neatly and added it to the pile. Then he came and sat down beside me. This was better! I had a chance. I reached for him, but he held me away.

"Suzanne, listen. We're not married. I'm free to go, and I'm going. You can have the apartment." Not for long; I couldn't pay the rent. "I'm wasting my talent; I'm wasting my time. I've got the world to explore. I've been cheating myself."

"What about Jason?" What about me?

"I didn't ask for Jason. He was your idea."

"That's true, Paul." Maybe if I was very humble. . . . "I admit that's true, but—"

"I never promised anything."

"I know. But, please, you don't have to go tonight. Stay one night; think it over."

"I've been thinking it over for a month. I'm going now. I'll send you money for Jason; I guess I owe you that."

"Paul—"

Jason woke up. He didn't cry or anything; he just scrabbled at the sides of his basket; and that was it. Paul leaped up and threw the shirts into his suitcase.

"Paul, where are you going?"

"Somewhere I've never been before! If I knew where, I wouldn't tell you, Suzanne!"

Those were our last words. Paul threw a searching look

around the apartment, making sure he hadn't forgotten anything. (He did forget the photos I had hung. He never even noticed I had hung them, or cleaned up, or anything.) Then he left.

Jason heard the door shut. He called out softly, then louder. Then he began to cry. LUV sang "I Can't Believe It," and I couldn't! I sat there not believing, refusing to believe that I was alone in an apartment whose rent was due, without money, without work, without a family, without friends, without Paul, with Jason.

January 5, Dawn

I wake in the dark. It must be very early, Jason lies asleep. I feel him breathing beside me. His soft breaths remind me of those flowers Mom used to plant along our edge of Jackson Street—wee white flower sprays. I lie very still next to Jason's warmth, feeling those flowers of breath on my hand. He must not wake till I have remembered my dream.

DREAM

It was the garden. Yes, I can see it now—that garden so much brighter than any garden I have ever seen. Slowly I walked through the long grass, trying not to crush the hidden flowers. Heavy seeds brushed against my gown. They clung and fell.

On the red-cushioned seat by the waterfall a woman rested. Her shield bore the female device, ♀ . Her gown flowed and shone like water, and it was embroidered with berries, wine-red. Gravely she looked at me; quietly she watched me come to her. I stood before her, and happiness hurt my heart, for she was my mother. I held out my arms to her, but I could not speak, and she did

not speak; she only raised her eyes to mine. In one
hand she lifted toward me the scepter tipped with
a ball; and I understood that this ball was our
human world.

A car rumbles in the street; headlights veer across the
ceiling. Jason whimpers and sucks his thumb. I pat him
very lightly on his soft, round tummy, and he quiets.
The woman is not my mother.
I think I know who the woman is.

January 5, 9:00 A.M.

Early on this cloudy blowy morning, we climb Aunt Millie's porch steps. I have been lugging Jason and Dada, a heavy, squirmy package. But now Jason insists on walking up the steps, waving Dada. Does he want to appear dignified, like a person instead of a package? For he knows where we're going. Aunt Millie has sometimes baby-sat for him. He likes her. And he knows if I leave him with her, I'll be back soon.

I ring the bell. Silence answers.

There's no light on inside, either, though the morning is dark.

But there has to be someone home! A house as thoroughly lived in as this one can never be empty! I ring again.

Now I hear a faint voice like a cat, crying. It's Little Eagle. It goes on and on. Should I break in, see what's happening? Can he be crying all by himself in an empty house? Of course not! Here come footsteps—fast, light footsteps, not Aunt Millie's. Harry peeps out the side window.

His thin face is pale. When he cracks the door open, I see his eyes are red. Why isn't he in school? Why is the living room behind him so dim and . . . dirty? I glimpse a roll of dust, a lampshade askew. Little Eagle wails louder.

Harry looks at me angrily. "Whatcha want?"

What does he think I want—to play marbles? "I'd like to see Aunt Millie." Beside me, Jason suddenly sounds off. Maybe he's answering Little Eagle; maybe he just feels the strangeness haunting the house behind Harry. I pick him up and get kicked in the hip.

"You can't," says Harry.

I don't believe this! "What?"

"She's sick."

As I hear these words, Jason gains ten pounds. I feel strength draining out of me along with hope. Halfheartedly I ask, "Can I do something?"

"Nope."

"Can I see her anyway, just for a minute?"

"She's in the hospital." Tears well out of Harry's red eyes.

Hospital! "What happened?"

"She fell down, couldn't talk. Uncle Stan called the amb'lance." Frankly crying, Harry shuts the door in my face.

I know what that means. Brendan Kelley fell down and couldn't talk, and they took him to the hospital. Dad said he had a stroke. Brendan Kelley died.

For a full minute I stand there, holding Jason, listening to Little Eagle, refusing to cry myself. Then I set Jason down and hand him Dada, whom he had dropped. "You walk now," I tell him. "I can't carry you all over creation." Jason throws Dada away and roars. Sighing, I pick them both up.

I'll just have to carry them all the way up Main to the bus station. It's not all that far, maybe four blocks. But my heart sinks at the thought of the wind and slush and ice from here to there!

I stuff Dada into my coat pocket. Jason won't walk, but he doesn't want to be carried, either. He arches his back and howls as I pick our way up Main. Big tears roll down his cheeks and freeze. People passing look at us curiously, with disgust. I know what they're thinking: "There's a horrid example of child abuse! What mother would leave a baby with a mean big sister like that one!"

There is nothing to do now, no way to go but Rianna's way. Harry closed more than the door of 70 Main in my face; he closed the last door. Now I am going to the station to buy one ticket to South Beach, California, one way. What would all these disgusted people say if they knew *that!*

I will not stay here. Sandwich wrappers blow by me. A stripped Christmas tree rolls downwind, streaming tinsel. People hurry past, heads down, careful of the ice. Even before they notice the disgusting spectacle of us, their faces are drawn in tense, anxious lines. *I want out.*

The Queen of Swords rules the world. The Empress is dead, or in the hospital, or has gone away, address unknown. My world is a motherless place where lost children wander; and I am one of the children.

Here is the station at last. I set Jason down on his feet, and he plunks right down on the grimy floor and won't budge. I try to pull him up, but it's like pulling a yowling rag doll. I am fearfully embarrassed. Lounging men look at us around their newspapers. A slim woman in furs and high heels turns around to gaze, and purses pink-frosted lips. Behind the counter, under the lush Bahamas poster, the watching clerk keeps his fat face smooth.

"OK," I say softly, furiously, to Jason. "Stay here if you want." And I walk away to the counter. I actually walk off a good ten yards and leave Jason sitting by himself on a filthy floor among strangers' legs and newspapers! I have never done this before. We have never been more than a foot apart in a public place.

Will these people remember? When Jason appears in the paper—*Is this your pooch?*—will they tell the police about the horrible older sister who left the kid crying in the station?

Will the clerk say, "Her? Oh, she bought a ticket to South Beach, California"?

It doesn't matter. Mary Alden has the Design School address anyhow.

The clerk makes the transaction extra quietly, barely muttering the few necessary words. He doesn't want to speak to me. The loudest sound in the station is Jason's howling. The clerk keeps his face smooth, but it hardens rapidly. I feel my face turning hard, too—hard like Rianna's.

January 5, 11:45 A.M.

"You want breakfast?" Rianna asks. She is just getting up. Opening the door to us she zips up her skirt, a floppy red one. Her hair runs wild down her back. She takes a second look at us. "Has the sky fallen in?"

"Jason's exhausted." He is out cold in my arms. I'm pretty tired myself. "Can I put him on your bed?"

"Go ahead." Rianna brushes her hair as I carry Jason behind the screen. Her narrow unmade bed is still warm. I lay him there, cover him, and blot frozen tears from his cheeks with a corner of sheet. "But we have to eat fast, Sue, I've got a client coming at noon, and I'm not centered yet."

I know Rianna does a special meditation thing called centering before a paid reading. It takes at least fifteen minutes. But I'm not leaving here till we get my life ironed out. The time has come to be selfish—frankly and all the way!

I help Rianna spread her velvet cloth and dust Isis. We open the Offering box and bait it with a five-dollar bill. Hopefully the client will be embarrassed to offer less.

Breakfast at Rianna's is, as I feared, not very exciting. After my trip to the bus station and to welfare and back, lugging Jason and Dada, I could happily wrap myself around a small pizza with anchovies! What I get is a half cup of cottage cheese with orange juice and brewer's yeast. We stand at the sink, nibbling and sipping; and Rianna keeps glancing at the clock.

I say, "I'm doing it your way."

Rianna shrugs. Her shrug says, Is there another way?

"I tried Aunt Millie. Rianna, she . . . she's had a stroke."

Sorrow softens Rianna's eyes for a moment. Then she says, "Her own fault. I told her. Years of refined flour and sugar."

"Do you have any sugar for this? Never mind—Rianna, what shall I do? I can't leave Jason in a supermarket, I can't!"

Jason lies sprawled under the blanket, one chubby hand at his cheek. His soft, tear-blotched face is turned away. I know I can't leave him frightened, searching among strangers for his Zu. I felt bad enough leaving him ten yards behind in the bus station!

Rianna is brisk. "OK. Leave him in your room, and I'll find him for you."

"When?"

"While you're getting on the bus. When is that?"

"Seven twenty."

"*A.M.?*" That opens her eyes!

"A.M."

"Hell! I'd only do it for you, Sue! OK, you walk out of there six forty-five; I'll find him seven thirty. I'll have him over to Family Service when they open, nine o'clock."

"What'll you say?"

"No problem. I heard him yelling; you were gone, I haven't a notion where."

"He'll wake up! He wakes me up!"

"Hell, why don't you just leave him off with me? They'll never know. And so what if they did! Look, Sue, the client's coming; I have to center."

I'm happier with that. Jason knows Rianna, even if he doesn't especially like her. He'll think I'm coming back.

Rianna rinses her plastic bowl and starts winding her

124

turban. "Don't worry about him, Sue. He'll forget you in a week; he's just a *baby*, hell!"

This is not all that reassuring: I don't want to be forgotten in a week. In spite of the half cup of cottage cheese, I feel empty. I stand there in my size-14 jeans and feel skinny. A wind blows through me.

Someone knocks. The client. "Hell," Rianna whispers, "I never centered!" She flies to open the door, red skirt flapping.

I go to gather up my sleeping Jason. When I turn back, the client is in the room. She is a large, middle-aged woman, surprisingly chic for a tarot client. Rianna helps her out of her real (?) fur coat as I sidle past, smiling apology.

Things Remembered

A MONTH AGO

On a strangely bright morning in early December, Jason and I crossed Main Street to the post office. I asked for Rianna's mail, and then, just in case, I asked for my own mail. And I had a letter!

I rested Jason on my hip and looked at the long, narrow envelope that came from the South Beach School of Design. Then I stuffed it into my coat pocket along with Rianna's bills and ads.

Vaguely I remembered sending a painting to the South Beach scholarship contest back last winter. Paul had just walked out on us then, and I was hunting around hopefully—not yet desperately—for a new life. Back then I had grand notions. Now I knew better. I was pretty sure what sort of form letter that envelope held!

I hoisted Jason to rest against my shoulder, patted the mail firmly down in my pocket, and set out across Main to State. The morning was brilliant with unhoped-for sunshine. Early Christmas shoppers almost sauntered from store to store. Coats swung carelessly open; people held doors for each other; passing cars flashed and glinted. The whole scene could have been a canvas titled *December Sunshine*, hung to brighten some quiet dim room.

Jason reached his little hands out to all this light and chuckled and laughed. I trudged down State in what Mom would call a brown study, seeing the bright world as if through a glass darkly. The sunshine hit my eyes but not my brain. My heart felt heavier than Jason, and carrying them both down State seemed almost more than I could do.

Last spring when the rent came due again, we moved out of Number 10 Sunfield. I was lucky to find this cheap room on State! We came there with the radio and hot plate, the mattress and box of clothes. (I had sold my good clothes to Thrift, which is why I now wear nothing but jeans.) We lived there on welfare, alone together.

Jason's colic saved us from that awful aloneness. I *think* it was colic. He cried for two nights and a day while I paced the floor with him, patting up bubbles and trying to shush him before some sleepless neighbor beat our door down. Number 114 is not soundproof. The second morning a neighbor did knock.

"Who is it?" I called through the door. I was exhausted, and a little scared. We knew no one at 114 State, or anywhere else.

"I live downstairs," said a young female voice.

Relieved, I opened the door to Rianna. She swept in like a fairy godmother in a long, flowing blue gown, with a bunch of herbs for a wand. When her herb tea had calmed Jason and he slept, she passed her hands over his stomach, up and down with weird gestures. "I'm a witch," she told me, smiling. "I do some healing."

She healed Jason, or the herbs did, or the thing ran its course. Anyhow I didn't have to take him to the doctor.

I was overjoyed to talk with another woman! Rianna came in as my fairy godmother and stayed as my friend, and before long I thought of her as a sister. I guess I clung to her a bit, which must have riled her, for Rianna stands on her own two feet and expects you to do the same. But she did not push me away. She lent a hand to pull me out of my muddy depression, and her friendship made my life possible again. But I thought nothing would ever bring back the excited joy I used to feel just because the sun was shining.

So on that bright December morning I dragged hopelessly down State, bringing Rianna's mail. I hauled it out of my pocket and dumped it on the table. Two cups were laid.

"You want tea?" Rianna asked. "It's ready. Hey, Sue, you got a letter!"

"Oh, yes." I picked it up.

"It's from that design place!"

"Yes."

"Aren't you going to open it?"

"I know what it says."

"The hell you do, without looking!"

I lifted the envelope to my forehead. "The vibes are coming through. This letter says . . . let me see . . . it says, 'Dear Ms. O'Hara, we regret to inform you that your painting, *Jason Wakes*, was declared dead on arrival!'"

Rianna laughed. Very suddenly she sobered. "Sue! Remember your last reading?"

No, I didn't remember it. I had so little hope I hardly noticed what the cards said.

"The Wheel of Fortune, remember? I said you would get a letter that would change your life."

"Oh, yes." I remembered that nonsense!

"Well, here it is. This is it! Give it to me!" Rianna snatched the letter. "I'll open it myself if you won't."

"Go ahead."

Rianna slit the envelope open with a spoon handle and unfolded the letter. Jason squeaked in my arms, reaching toward the crackling paper. Over his head I watched Rianna light up and smile. "Just like I said! Read it!"

She handed me my letter. Holding it away from Jason, I read, "Dear Ms. O'Hara, I am most happy to inform you that your picture, *Jason Wakes*, has been awarded first prize in our Scholarship Contest. . . ."

When I read it over, it seemed to say the same thing. I sat down at the table and let Jason slide down to sit on my feet. I read the letter again. Each time I read it I got the same message. "Your picture has been awarded first prize in our Scholarship Contest. . . ."

Jason whimpered, plucking at my jeans. Rianna hummed as she poured tea.

Then it hit me. I had won the contest. I had a full scholarship, with room and board, at South Beach Design, starting in January.

Sunshine zoomed in the window and zonked the cups till they gleamed like snow. Rianna's rare smile shone. I lifted Jason and his soft skin smelled like roses. For months the world had been dark for me. Now the sun hurt my eyes! I laughed for joy and kissed Jason. Rianna bent to me, and I kissed her. She said, "One thing. What are you going to do with Jason?"

"I don't know, I'll think of something." But not right then; I was much too excited!

"You only have till January. That's not much time."

"I can pack in five minutes!" Three.

"I mean, to do something with Jason."

"Oh, Jason, sure. Don't look like that, Rianna! I've got a whole month!"

It would take me more than a month to float down from my rainbow to earth again. Even now, if I just say to myself "I won the scholarship," I start floating back up. Way down there I see the black hole I was in a month ago. That was no good for either of us, Jason or me. Sooner or later I would have started hitting him, knocking him around out of sheer misery. For both our sakes I must never sink down there again!

But now it's a month later, and I still haven't figured out about Jason.

Now there's only one thing to be done about Jason.

January 5, Night

Jason and I feast together. Sitting on our mattress I feed him his favorite applesauce and a spoonful of my lasagna. He takes one lick at that and turns his head away! He lies back with his aba, smiling sweetly at me. The radio sings sweetly. I feel sick.

But I don't mind polishing off the lasagna myself. If I had another can of lasagna or ravioli or spaghetti or chili, I'd open it now for comfort. I feel very thin tonight, and my throat's choked up so I can't breathe right.

I set the alarm for six. For the last time I lie down under the sleeping bag with Jason and Dada. Jay breathes down my neck, those soft breaths like Mom's flowers. He holds onto my wrist and nuzzles me. I am his Zuzu, his safety. It's a great thing entirely that he doesn't guess how weak and scared I am. It's a great thing altogether kids never know that about their folks. I always felt perfectly safe with Mom; she was solid earth to me. If I'd known the truth of her, I'd have died of fright.

Jason doesn't imagine I'm leaving him. He may never see me again, *never again*, but he hasn't a gleam! Rianna says he'll forget me in a week. I hope—and fear—he will find another Zu; someone who will always be there, solid earth, the way I can't be. He'll forget me. He'll forget all of this—he's so young—as though it never happened. And he'll get a good Zu—please, God!

Out on State, trucks rumble by. Out by the bathroom, a couple quarrels; she shrills, he roars. I think I doze, between wakings.

Where is Mom tonight? Will she ever find out that I ran off and left her grandbaby alone in this cold civilized world? If so, will she ever speak to me again?

Holy Pat, it's all *her* fault! Where was she when I needed her?

I am all packed. My Christmas carryall stands in the corner, ready to go. I've packed two pairs of jeans, a sweatshirt, socks, undies, tampons, my sketch pad. In my pants pocket I've got $42.50, and my ticket. And those dollars are all for me! They won't go for applesauce or abas or disposables. I figure I'll eat nothing but milk till I get there. Just sitting, jouncing along on the bus, I won't need much. Maybe I'll get there thin—as well as rich!

I mustn't forget Dad's address. Put that in my coat pocket when I get up, first thing. Rianna can have the clock . . . and the radio . . . and the pictures off the wall. The only picture I packed is the portrait of Mom with her back turned. . . .

DREAM

I am on the bus, alone with Dada. Somehow he got stuffed in my coat pocket. I wish with all my heart I had left Dada behind; Jason will miss him. To me, he's just a pain. I pull him out of my pocket and throw him away.

The bus grinds to a stop. The driver turns around and looks at me; and he is the kind black man who helped me call my Dad from Ahmed's. He looks at me expectantly over people's heads,

132

and pretty soon all the heads turn and look at me. This is my stop.

I climb down, and the bus roars off without me.

But this is not South Beach, California! This is the garden. Sunny green it opens before me. I hear the waterfall burbling in the pure, quiet air.

Carefully I walk in the garden, so as not to crush the flowers. Seeds brush against my gown, and cling, and fall.

By the waterfall the red-cushioned seat is empty. Only the scepter rests on the cushions. I look long at the shield, and its device, ♀ . At last I take up the scepter, and sink down on the red cushions.

Calmly I glance about the quiet garden, where seed-heavy grasses wave in the wind. My lap is clothed in rippling white, red-embroidered. My gown flows like the waterfall. Stars fall from my hair and shine in my lap. In my hand, the world scepter sways heavily. The voice of the waterfall deepens.

January 6, Dawn

I am awake.

The room is so dark, so desperately cold, I know it must be six o'clock. That's what the clock says, gleaming whitely across the small mound of Jason—six on the dot. It murmurs, ready to ring. I reach over and snap it off.

Very gently I turn back the sleeping bag and slip off the mattress. In the dark, teeth chattering, I dive into pants and sweater and run out to the bathroom. I shake and shiver, but only with cold. Inside I am strong.

Back in our room I flick on the overhead light and start rolling Jason's stuff into a ball. The red sweater he can wear, and the elephant-patch pants, and of course, his jacket and cap. Everything else gets rolled small-small-small and crushed into the carryall. Three shirts, four rubber pants, six disposables—can I buy those at bus stations?—three denim pants, the aba. The aba won't fit; anyhow, I'll want it handy. I drop it into my coat pocket. There's room there for several more disposables, scrunched. And Dada? Dada lies on his back, thrown off the mattress. I see myself carrying my baggage under one arm, Jason under the other, and Dada in my teeth. How will I pull out and present my ticket?

Under the harsh light Jason stirs. He yawns, wide and pink, stretches, opens his eyes. A moment he glances around, surprised to find himself alone on the huge mattress. Then he sees me where I kneel, hopelessly working Dada between disposables. And he smiles. Jason smiles like the baby Jesus in a Christmas crèche and holds out his arms to me. "Um, Zuzu," he says. "Um!"

Jason wakes to his cold, ugly world, and he sees me and smiles. He knows he's safe with his Zuzu. And he's right; by God, he's right!

For I am The Empress. The world must have an Empress; without her, there is no garden; without the garden, there is no light. If my world is loveless, then I must be love. If my house is motherless, then I must be the mother. I myself am the calm Empress in the quiet garden. And I thought I was The Queen of Swords! But I carry no sword. I carry the world.

Jason struggles to sit up. "Zu," he says. "Aba."

"Not now," I tell him. "When we get on the bus." I remember to stuff Dad's address into my other coat pocket. I'll keep in touch with Dad, and one day Mom will call, or drop in on one of us; I know she will! And then I'll be able to look her in the face, which I sure couldn't do if I had abandoned her grandbaby.

"Zu?"

"Mama. Can you say Mama, Jason?"

Sure he can! He's been wanting to say it, but I wouldn't answer to it. "Maaaa-ma!" He grins.

Loud and sudden, a knock on our door. I open to Rianna—a most unusual Rianna, unkempt, dim-eyed, dressed in faded pajamas under a crumpled caftan. She sees smiling Jason. She sees me holding Dada. She asks, "What in hell are you doing?"

"Packing us."

"Sue, you're cracked! You can't haul that kid across the country on a bus!"

135

"Let's get dressed," I say to Jason. "Time to go bye-bye."

He chuckles as I change him. Rianna stands over us, tight-faced.

"What about bottles? How are you going to heat them?"

"He'll have to drink cold."

"How will you keep it cold?"

"We'll manage." I'll buy a thermos.

"What about applesauce? What about *disposables?*"

"I know it's not going to be a picnic—"

"You bet your life!"

"But we'll manage. We're in it together." I wrestle Jason's arms into his shirtsleeves and pull the red sweater over his head. He laughs at Rianna while I search for his hands and draw them into the sleeves. "Um, Zuzu," he explains to her. "Mama." And he's right.

I draw the elephant pants up him and wriggle on socks and shoes. I jostle him into his jacket. "You're in orbit!" says Rianna. "You're swinging by your tail!"

"Um," says Jason. "Bye-bye." I boggle at him. That's a brand-new word just popped out of that pink mouth, and at the appropriate moment! And not a minute too soon, says the clock.

I stand up and shrug into my bulging coat. "Bye-bye," Jason shouts triumphantly, lifting his arms. I pick him up. "It's just Dada," I mumble to Rianna, "I can't fit him in."

She picks Dada off the floor and dusts him. "Does Jason have a pocket?"

"Good thought!"

She slips Dada up to his arms into Jason's coat pocket. Then she pushes the carryall into the sleeping bag and zips up the whole mess. "Better you than me!" she says. And she darts at me, and kisses me awkwardly on the forehead.

We must go. But I set Jason down once more and throw my arms around Rianna. In all my heart confusion I never

136

realized till this moment that I was leaving my sister be-hind.

When I let her go, I see she's weeping. Transparent tears soften her dark eyes. Astonished, I whisper, "Rianna?"

She says, "I have to tell you."

"Tell me what?" I'm picking Jason up, and the sleeping bag. Already I feel like a tired camel, and we haven't even started the walk to the station!

"I have a message for you."

"Rianna—" There is no more talking time.

"A letter. It came yesterday, special delivery. I signed."

"Let's have it!"

"It's from Family Service. . . ." Rianna hikes the caftan and searches her pajama pockets. "All it says, they're open-ing a branch office or something in South Beach. You can call this number. . . ."

Rianna read my letter. Holy Pat, she steamed it open and read it and stuck it in her pocket! Well, so why am I shocked? Rianna makes her own rules; I've always known that.

She fishes a wad of paper out of a pocket and jams it into mine on top of Dad's address. "There's the number. You call, and they'll do something about Jason. Sue, can you ever forgive me?"

In Rianna's tear-brimming eyes I see the country of The Queen of Swords. Rianna lives there alone with her memories. I know who they are. There's Carl, who left her, and the baby she aborted, and the baby who toddled away in the supermarket, and a crowd of foster parents; and I myself was almost there.

"I wasn't going to tell you," Rianna confesses. "I guess . . . I don't know, maybe. . . ."

"I know," I tell her simply, truthfully. "I see." If I had rushed off and left my Jason behind, Rianna would have had me with her in that dark country. We would have lived there together, she and I, forever. "You've told me now," I comfort her. "Thanks for telling me now."

Rianna wraps her arms around Jason and me and the sleeping bag, and we stand swaying together. She doesn't say, "I'm sorry." I don't say, "I understand." We don't say, "I love you," or even "Good-bye." We just stand close together.

January 6, 7:30 A.M.

We barely make the bus. At half past seven we are roaring out of town toward the turnpike. Jason and Dada sprawl on the inside seat, watching storefronts and black snowbanks jog past. Bent figures, huddled against the cold, step cautiously on ice. Sad faces wait at a local bus stop. Gray light seeps into the city.

The bus shifts gears and speeds up. We mount a long ramp that curves up to the east-west turnpike. The city drops away. Streetlights still glow among its dark snowbanks; a crown of smoke hangs over its roofs. Ahead and around, snowfields spread far and far. They are whiter than clean, ironed sheets that smell of sunshine. They are whiter than purity.

East, above the city rim, the sun rises. Red light spills across the world, painting snow and sky with a rich, glowing wash. Even west, where we turn, the snowfields gleam.

F
CROMPTON Crompton, Anne Eliot

Queen of swords

524589

DATE DUE

2-15 88			
6.7.88			